"There's something else you can keep me from." Ryan grinned.

Anna rested her hand on top of her basketball-size stomach. "What's that?"

"You can keep me from another Friday night of eating alone." He winked at her. "Dinner will give us a chance to catch up. Our Christmas reunion. A lot has happened since we last saw each other."

"No kidding." Her gaze fell to the wooden steps. "I'm sorry about your dad, Ryan." She dropped her hand to her side. "Mateo was going through chemo and…"

"We lost touch. No problem. So…dinner?"

Her lashes feathered her skin. "I never could say no to you."

Which wasn't how he remembered high school. Though more often than not, he hadn't given her a chance to say no. He'd been too scared to ask Anna to prom or on a date. He'd reckoned it best to be content being best friends. But how many times had he secretly wished for more…

Lisa Carter and her family make their home in North Carolina. In addition to her Love Inspired novels, she writes romantic suspense for Abingdon Press. When she isn't writing, Lisa enjoys traveling to romantic locales, teaching writing workshops and researching her next exotic adventure. She has strong opinions on barbecue and ACC basketball. She loves to hear from readers. Connect with Lisa at lisacarterauthor.com.

Books by Lisa Carter

Love Inspired

Coast Guard Courtship
Coast Guard Sweetheart
Falling for the Single Dad
The Deputy's Perfect Match
The Bachelor's Unexpected Family
The Christmas Baby

The
Christmas Baby

Lisa Carter

HARLEQUIN® LOVE INSPIRED®

Recycling programs
for this product may
not exist in your area.

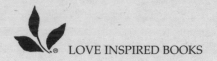 **LOVE INSPIRED BOOKS**

ISBN-13: 978-0-373-62318-1

The Christmas Baby

www.Harlequin.com

Printed in U.S.A.

Now before the Feast of the Passover,
Jesus knew that His hour had come that
He would depart out of this world to the Father,
having loved His own who were in the world,
He loved them to the end.
—*John* 13:1

This book is dedicated to my late uncle, Hugh Adams. You are missed. Thank you for sharing your family with me. I will always treasure the memories of fun, golf and barbecue chicken.

But most of all, thank you for Christmas.

Chapter One

His footsteps echoing, Ryan Savage walked the first grader from the cafeteria toward the media center. The dismissal bell had released the rest of the students to buses and to car pool thirty minutes ago.

Oscar's hand slipped into Ryan's. "Mister Sabbage?" The child barely spoke above a whisper.

Biting back a smile, Ryan paused in the school corridor. "What is it, Oscar? Are you still hungry?"

Eligible students enrolled in the after-school tutoring program received a healthy snack. For some of them, it was the only food they'd receive until returning to school the next morning for a nutritious breakfast.

Small for his age, the little boy shook his head. "I jus' wonnered if the new teacher in our group was as nice as Miz Thompson. I'm gonna miss her."

There was something endearing about the child, which tugged at Ryan's heart. "Perhaps Mrs. Thompson will return to school after she has her baby. But I think you'll like the teacher who is taking her place."

"What's her name?"

"Mrs. Reyes is an old friend of mine." Ryan smiled.

"In fact, we became best friends when we were in first grade like you."

This was Anna's first day of teaching at the small elementary school outside Kiptohanock, Virginia, where they'd grown up. He was looking forward to seeing her again, but an unexpected nervousness opened in the pit of his stomach. Which was ridiculous. He wasn't the gangly teenager who once had feelings for Anna Pruitt.

Oscar's eyes widened. "You were in first grade like me?"

Ryan rolled his tongue in his cheek. "Hard to believe, I know. But true."

Oscar shook his head as if he wasn't quite sure he should believe Ryan. "Is she pwetty?"

Ryan pushed his glasses farther along the bridge of his nose. "I think so. You'll have to tell me what you think."

Oscar nodded. "We better go see."

Anna was probably already inside the media center waiting with the other two students who would make up their group in the after-school enrichment program.

Pressing through the doors, Ryan steered Oscar past other clumps of students and supervising adults. The intervention teams were composed of teachers, professional counselors and trained community volunteers.

Due to a poor attendance record, Oscar was falling behind his classmates. His classroom teacher also reported that when Oscar managed to get to school, he often fell asleep. A six-year-old shouldn't be so tired. Ryan needed to make a home visit to talk with Oscar's mother.

Weaving past the computer lab and waist-high bookcases, Ryan waved to other kids he'd come to know during his short career as a fifth-grade teacher. Students entered the program due to behavioral issues and low academic performance in math or language. The goal was to help kids rise above difficult home circumstances and acquire the academic and lifestyle skills to achieve success far beyond their current situations.

Sighting Anna's dark hair at one of the tables, he herded Oscar forward. But the knot of apprehension in Ryan's gut tightened.

Until they went off-Shore to college and lost touch, they'd been best friends. While he'd pursued a research career, she eventually married someone else. A marine.

Now as a young military widow, Anna had just returned home. Hired by the school board to finish the term for a kindergarten teacher on maternity leave till after Christmas. And only this week, Principal Carden asked Ryan to head an additional support team for three newly identified at-risk kids.

On this late November afternoon, the light spilled milky sunshine through the blinds on the window and across the table where Anna and a little girl hunkered over a picture book.

Ryan stopped short, his hand on Oscar's shoulder. His heart was in his throat—which as a scientist he knew to be an anatomical impossibility and yet at this moment it was proven true.

Anna's long hair lay gathered across one shoulder, secured by a clip. Beneath the quilted, white vest, she wore a red-and-black-striped flannel plaid shirt. Red—like Christmas, he remembered—was her favorite.

Her finger skimmed underneath the line of words on the printed page. Her voice as soft and melodious as ever, as she occasionally prompted the little girl reading aloud.

But he couldn't catch a glimpse of Anna's dark brown eyes. His pulse ratcheted. When she glanced up, would she be pleased or indifferent to see him?

Oscar surged toward the cluster of chairs around the

table. And when her eyes fastened onto Ryan, Anna gave a soft gasp.

Ryan held himself motionless. "Hello, Anna."

The corners of her mouth curved. And a light appeared in those melted chocolate eyes of hers. Warming at the sight of him. "Ryan."

Oscar's blue eyes darted from Ryan to Anna. "I thought his name was Mister Sabbage."

She laughed. Like the sound of tinkling wind chimes on a gentle ocean breeze.

"It is Mr. Savage, Oscar." He ruffled the hair on top of the little boy's head, and Oscar smiled. A cautious smile. As if unused to affection. Or trust. Ryan could relate.

Oscar plopped into a chair. "You're right, Mister Sabbage. She is very pwetty."

She blushed.

"Thank you, Oscar." She extended her hand across the table. "I'm Mrs. Reyes. And I am so happy to meet you. I hope we'll have fun together after school."

Oscar gave her fingers a quick squeeze. Then laying his head on the table, he closed his eyes.

Ryan pulled out a chair across from Anna. He recognized the little girl, Maria Guzman. Overweight compared to her second-grade peers, she could speak and understand English according to her file, but her reading ability was below grade level.

Sixty-something Agnes Parks headed their way with the third student in tow, Zander Benoit. Mrs. Parks was the wife of Ryan's pastor. Their daughter, Darcy, had once been Anna's best girl friend in high school.

Throwing himself into one of the empty seats, third grader Zander held himself taut. But his black eyes never stopped moving, assessing the other children, the room and Ryan, too. He wasn't sure why, but Zander reminded

Ryan of his brother, Ethan, who'd just returned home from the army.

When the child's gaze landed on the red Exit sign, Ryan understood the connection between his combat veteran brother and the third grader. Zander was formulating an exit strategy. Calculating the distance between the table and the door. The way Ryan was planning his own exit strategy after Christmas.

"What's with the candy canes, man?"

Ryan's attention snapped to Zander. A diversionary tactic? As if he sensed Ryan getting too close. Zander deserved a home visit, too.

Oscar's eyes opened, and he lifted his head. Maria glanced around the media center walls, decorated with candy cane cutouts. The week after Thanksgiving, a few industrious colleagues had begun the holiday countdown to winter break.

Zander jutted his jaw. "Do we get candy after this boring school thing is done?" Behavioral issues had landed Zander in the program.

Ryan leaned back in his chair. "No candy. But—" he made sure he had everyone's attention "—if each of you complete your weekly goals, we have a big reward planned for the group before winter break."

Oscar's face lit. "We get Chwistmas?"

"Don't be stupid," Zander responded before Ryan could. "Christmas isn't real."

Oscar's face fell.

Maria stuck out her chin. "*Estupido* is a bad word. Isn't it, Mrs. Reyes?"

Anna laid her palms on the tabletop. "We don't say stupid, Zander."

"Whatever." Zander thrust out his chest. "But Christmas is for babies."

Ryan shook his head. "That's not true, Zander. Christmas is for everyone."

He threw Anna an apologetic look. They hadn't had time to confer. "Mrs. Parks and I were thinking about a field trip next week to the tree lighting in the Kiptohanock town square."

Agnes Parks smiled. "With milkshakes and dinner beforehand. On us."

"Milkshakes?" Zander's dark eyes took on a gleam of interest.

Agnes nudged a math workbook toward him. "And the countdown to everyone reaching their goals begins right now."

Ryan had his own private countdown. After Christmas, he was returning to the pharmaceutical position he'd abandoned to come home and help his family when his father died.

Yet surprisingly, Ryan had enjoyed the last three years as a fifth-grade teacher. A job far different from the technical work for which he'd trained. And even more of a surprise, he'd relished the opportunity to make a difference in the lives of at-risk kids like Maria, Oscar and Zander. Although with a tough kid like Zander, how much a difference he made remained to be seen.

Zander's eyes slitted. "You mean them two—" his index finger jabbed the air "—got to meet their goals for *me* to get a chocolate milkshake?"

Mrs. Parks—whose team specialty included character building and cooperative learning—rested her slightly plump chin in her hand. "Exactly what we discussed earlier, Zander. We're here to help each other succeed."

Necessary in most endeavors, academic or otherwise. Crucial in life—as Ryan discovered when he and his siblings rallied to save the family business.

Mrs. Parks patted Zander's hand. "Zander is fabulous on the computer. He has a lot he can teach us."

Zander muttered under his breath. "How fun."

Ignoring him, Anna laid the picture book on the table. "Let's get started, shall we?"

Ryan's pulse accelerated. And although he understood she was speaking to the children, her smile was for him.

Anna Pruitt Reyes inhaled the familiar and comforting scents of the elementary school media center. The musty smell of books. The faint leftover aroma of coffee from the teachers' lounge.

It felt good to teach again. And after fourteen years, good to be home on the Eastern Shore, the narrow peninsula bordered by the Chesapeake Bay on the west and the Atlantic on the east.

Sweet, shy Maria headed off with Mrs. Parks to the computer lab. Zander feigned disinterest while Ryan attempted to show him how to subtract fractions.

Prodded awake, Oscar came over to Anna's side of the table. And a tender spot grew in her heart for the little guy in clean but ill-fitting blue jeans. Zander's ragged jacket was totally inadequate for the coming winter months. But though her clothes were from a discount store, Maria appeared cared for.

In her previous teaching post in Texas, Anna had enjoyed her after-school work with at-risk students. And now more than ever, she needed the salary supplement.

She worked with Oscar on sight words and phonetics. While he practiced writing the letters of the alphabet, she took the opportunity to get her first good look at Ryan.

He hadn't changed much. The same light brown hair. The eyeglasses were new, though, since she'd last seen him. He'd switched to contact lenses their senior year.

But apparently he'd gone back to wearing frames, which suited him.

A tie hung askew at the open collar of his blue Oxford dress shirt. In a pair of belted jeans and brown suede shoes, he looked very much like what he was—a schoolteacher. Except far too handsome compared to any schoolteacher she'd ever known.

Placing the textbook in Zander's backpack, Ryan's chest rippled with muscles beneath the brown blazer. No longer the endearing, if goofy, boy she remembered with such fondness.

She flushed when Ryan caught her staring. The awkward moment ended as another volunteer arrived to take the children to the transportation bus.

Ryan jumped to his feet. "Great work today, kids." Lanky as ever, he high-fived Maria and Oscar. Zander moved out of reach.

She straightened the books. "Have a great weekend, everyone."

Mrs. Parks gathered her handbag. "See you on Monday." The media center slowly emptied until only Anna and Ryan remained.

"It's good to see you, Anna. Welcome home."

Renewing her friendship with Ryan had factored in her decision to finally return home. And because of their friendship, she couldn't delay revealing the truth any longer. Scraping the chair across the carpet, she rose heavily to her feet.

His smile froze. Behind the brownish-black frames of his glasses, bewilderment dotted his eyes. Her heart skipped a beat. If her dearest friend in the world couldn't understand, how would her parents react?

Almost without intending to, she placed her palm over her abdomen. And his eyes—the blue-green of so many in seaside Kiptohanock—flickered at the movement of her hand.

His features had become carved of stone, all chiseled bone and rugged angles. "I didn't realize you'd remarried."

She took a quick, indrawn breath. "I haven't." And with those simple words, it began.

His jaw tightened. "I see." The stubble was new since high school. Giving him an attractive maturity. He looked away toward the window overlooking the playground.

She'd expected better from him. "What is it you think you see, Ryan?"

"I see a woman nine months preg—"

"Seven months." Heat mounted above her collar. All too aware she resembled a beached whale.

A muscle ticked in that strong, square-cut jaw of his. "A woman seven months pregnant. A widow for the last two—"

"Mateo died nearly three years ago from cancer."

"Who…?" Ryan cleared his throat. "Whose child is this?"

A child posthumously conceived from her late husband's stored sperm before Mateo began chemotherapy. But Anna was tired of explaining herself.

"Mine." She raised her chin. "The child is mine, Ryan."

He scrubbed the back of his neck. "I don't know what to say to you, Anna."

"Say that you're my friend." Her mouth trembled. "Say that you understand."

"But I don't understand, Anna. Why are you— What did your dad say when you got home?"

Her eyes dropped to the floor. But because of her protruding belly, she could no longer see her black flats. "Dad and Mom are still at the army base with Jaxon in Europe. They don't know yet."

"You haven't told them?" He gestured at her stomach. "Not exactly something you can hide."

"I'm not hiding." She bit her lip. Not anymore.

His broad shoulders slumped. "I was sorry to hear about Jax's wife."

"Exactly why I haven't told my parents. They'll be home after New Year's."

Who could've foreseen that she and her older brother, Jaxon, would both be widowed? This first Christmas without his wife, Jax needed their parents' support. Their undivided attention.

She wasn't eager to face the disappointment in her beloved father's eyes. A disappointment not unlike the look on Ryan's face.

"How did Charlie take the news?"

Charlie was Anna's youngest brother, a deputy sheriff in town.

She pursed her lips. "I haven't told him yet. I drove straight across the Bay Bridge Tunnel to school this morning from Virginia Beach."

"Did you stay overnight with Will?" Ryan's brow creased. "What did he say?"

A year younger than Anna, her firefighter brother lived on the other side of the bay.

"I made him promise to let me tell the rest of the family in my own time."

Ryan shook his head. "So you drove all the way from Texas? You must be exhausted, Anna."

In more ways than he could possibly know. Yet she was compelled by an inexplicable need to come home and mend fences with her family.

She took a breath. "I called Charlie this morning to let him know I was driving straight to work."

Ryan frowned. "As I recall, your ex–deputy sheriff father doesn't like surprises. Are you sure springing the baby on them is the best way to handle the situation?"

She tucked a tendril of hair behind her ear. "I wish you'd trust I've made the best decision for me and my baby."

His eyes locked onto hers. "I wish…"

Something fluttered inside her chest. What did he wish?

He pinched his lips together. "Never mind." Pivoting, he exited the media center as suddenly as he'd reappeared in her life.

She blinked away tears. "Merry Christmas to you, too."

Why had she believed it would be different here? Brushing aside every obstacle, she'd left everything behind to be home for Christmas. She'd so needed a new start.

If this was any indication of the reception she'd get from her hometown… Her gut wrenched. She'd hoped the people who knew her best and loved her the most would also love this child.

Had she made a mistake in coming home?

Chapter Two

Out in the school parking lot, Ryan regretted his abrupt departure. He wrenched open his car door. There were so many questions he should've asked Anna. But he'd been stunned by her pregnancy.

Where was the baby's father? Why had he left Anna to face her family alone with the news? What kind of man—?

His gut tightened. What sort of friend was he to let her face her family alone? She'd only asked one thing of him. To be her friend. To trust her.

But the pregnancy made no sense. This wasn't like Anna. Not the Anna Pruitt he remembered. After her husband's death, had she succumbed to grief or loneliness? Had she changed so much from those long-ago childhood days?

Getting into his car, he drove toward town. He followed Highway 13, which bisected the Delmarva Peninsula of Delaware, Maryland and Virginia into bayside and seaside. The tiny fishing village of Kiptohanock—their hometown—hugged the Atlantic shoreline.

Entering the small hamlet, he looped around the village square. The Waterman's Association had been busy.

Christmas wreaths hung from the gas-powered lanterns on each corner of the green.

Anna's sister-in-law, Evy, worked in the library on the west side. On the south end of the square stood the white brick volunteer fire department. Ryan parked in the empty parking lot of the Sandpiper Cafe, closed for the evening.

This time of year, he found himself missing his father more than usual. His dad had loved participating in community events.

On the nearby waterfront, commercial and recreational boats bobbed in the marina. The steeple of the white clapboard church pierced the winter sky above the harbor. At the Coast Guard station, flags fluttered in the stiff wind.

The wind off the water would be cold this time of year. Yet his oceanside home rarely saw snow nor, hopefully, none of the more usual ice storms.

What kind of Christmas did Oscar, Maria or Zander look forward to? In less than a month, he'd say goodbye to his classroom and the kids forever.

His hands clenched around the wheel. Which was what he'd worked for—to leave the family on a better financial footing and return to the research he loved.

But the children he'd leave behind tugged at his heart. Even Zander, despite the third grader's determination to keep everyone at arm's length. Ryan blew out a breath of air. He'd not foreseen that when he tendered his resignation.

Arm's length. He'd done the same since changing careers and coming home to help his family. As for seeing Anna again? The rush of emotion had caught Ryan by surprise.

What would happen to kids like Oscar, Maria and Zander after Ryan left the Shore for good?

He throttled the steering column. "This isn't my problem, God." But saying that out loud didn't ease his conscience as he'd hoped.

Ryan released his grip on the wheel and leaned against the seat. The replacement teacher would be fine. The children would be fine. Anna and her baby would be fine.

Would they? Would Ryan? Was there a reason Anna had come into his life now?

Only the sound of shorebirds wheeling above the glittering water of the inlet broke the silence. But he couldn't shake the memory of the unspoken plea in Anna's beautiful eyes. To trust her. To understand. To be her friend.

She seemed so sad and alone. First losing her husband and now being a single parent. He shouldn't have walked away. He needed to apologize. No one should feel that sad or alone, especially at Christmas.

And when her very intimidating ex-deputy dad found out about the baby... Ryan winced. He didn't envy Anna that conversation.

He spied Seth Duer stuffing something fur-lined and red into the cab of his truck, and Ryan got an idea. He grinned. A surprise not only for the children, but for Anna, too.

So like their deputy sheriff father, Charlie's uniformed shoulders hunched in the overstuffed armchair. "Why didn't you tell us about the baby, Anna?"

Sitting on the sofa in her childhood home, Anna fidgeted. "Because you would've tried to talk me out of it."

Perched on the armrest, Evy dangled her trademark high heels. "And your due date is January 6?" Her smile made her cheeks brush her retro horn-rimmed eyeglasses. "An Old Christmas baby. The Epiphany."

The glasses reminded Anna of Ryan. She'd expected too much from a childhood friend she hadn't seen in years.

She'd underestimated the distance time and geography had created between them.

Just before high school graduation, she'd actually thought—hoped—Ryan might care for her as more than a friend. But he never said anything. And she chalked it up to wishful thinking. The road not taken. At this point, a road she couldn't afford to take.

She steeled herself against the ache Ryan's rejection evoked. "Mateo's people call it the Día de Los Reyes."

"Reyes. 'Kings' in Spanish." Evy's blond ponytail swished. "The Magi. Three Kings' Day."

"A day of gifts." Anna locked eyes with her scowling brother. "And this child is his last, best gift to me."

His elbows on his knees, Charlie steepled his hands under his chin. "With the rest of the Pruitts scattered far and wide this Christmas, there's plenty of room for you at the house."

She looked at her brother with his Clark Kent good looks. "I appreciate the offer, but I rented a house on Quayside Lane before I left Texas."

His brow furrowed. "This is your home, Anna."

With her older brothers, Jaxon and Ben, on active military duty and firefighter Will on the mainland, it had fallen to Charlie to keep the home fires burning. A home where she'd spent a happy childhood.

Charlie frowned. "You don't have to do everything by yourself, Anna."

Evy slid onto the sofa beside Anna. "We want to be here for you."

Anna's gaze darted between them. "I love you both for your support, but it's better this way."

"Quayside is so remote." He lifted his chin, the cleft clearly visible. "It's not good for you to be out there alone. Especially with winter upon us."

"I'm the big sister, remember, Charlie? I'll be fine."

Anna glanced out the picture window at the maples lining the street. Having dropped the last of their leaves, the bare branches revealed the stark beauty of winter. Christmas used to be her favorite time of year.

She hardly remembered the girl she'd once been. Full of optimism as she headed off to college. Surprised by love's possibilities after meeting handsome Marine Corps PFC Reyes. And because of Mateo's deployment, a whirlwind wedding. The girl she'd been before death and fear took their toll.

"Why did you do this, Anna?" Her brother's pensive tone pulled her away from her memories. "Why not start a new family with someone else?"

She stiffened. "I want Mateo's child."

"His child keeps you mired in the past." Charlie's lips tightened. "You lost your teaching job over this, didn't you?"

She knotted her hands in her lap. "There were side effects with the fertility drugs. I was absent a lot." It was the understatement of the century. "The school district chose not to renew my contract. But I have to do this. This child is Mateo's legacy preserved forever."

"Do you hear yourself, Anna?" His eyes widened. "What kind of burden is that for a kid to bear? Being someone's memorial candle. How dare Mateo Reyes ask you to do this."

She stood so fast she swayed. "That's not how it was. I *want* to do this. I *need* to do this." She squared her shoulders. "I didn't go into this lightly."

"Help us to understand." Evy caught Anna's arm. "Please sit down."

She allowed Evy to pull her onto the sofa again. "Neither Mateo or I ever believed he wouldn't win the war against the cancer. He was so young. So strong. So full of life…" Her voice broke. "Don't you think I've considered what it will mean to bring a fatherless child into the world?"

Charlie came out of his chair and crouched in front of her. "Raising a child as a single mother is going to be so hard, sis." He reached for her hand.

"This was Mateo's greatest desire—to have a child."

Her brother's hazel eyes bored into hers. "There was a court case a few years ago, which made national headlines. Posthumous children aren't entitled to Social Security or military benefits. They have few legal rights." He blew out a breath.

Charlie didn't know the half of it. The procedure hadn't been covered by the VA. She didn't want her family to know how she'd depleted her savings.

"At first, I tried artificial insemination. But after three failed attempts—"

"You weren't pregnant at our wedding a year ago." Evy put her hand to her throat. "How long have you been trying to conceive, Anna?"

A question she preferred not to answer. "The good news is that the in vitro finally worked." After two failed procedures.

She'd sold anything she could live without. Everything she owned in the world sat in her VW Beetle parked in front of the house.

Charlie rocked on his heels. "Stay here, Anna. With people who love you."

She shook her head. "I need to do this on my own."

Evy's expressive blue eyes clouded. "Need or want?"

Anna chewed her bottom lip. "When Mrs. Savage forwarded the notice of the interim position so close to Christmas, I thought…"

Thanks to pregnancy hormones, she'd been weepy the day the email arrived. She'd given in to the growing desire to come home. To spend Christmas with those near and dear to her heart. But above all, to make a new life for her child.

And the kindergarten opening offered a small financial cushion to take the edge off her empty bank account. As she was learning, babies were expensive.

Charlie glanced at the mantel clock. "It's the middle of the night in Europe, but we can call Mom and Dad first thing—"

"I'm not ready to tell them yet." She fisted the hem of her vest.

"They deserve to know the truth."

"Please, Charlie. A few more weeks." She opened her palms on her lap. "Let me be the one to tell them."

Single parenting would be the ultimate and final letdown of everything they once hoped and dreamed for her.

He sighed. "But in the meantime, what will you say to people in town?"

In Kiptohanock, everybody was always up in everybody else's business.

She sniffed. "Why should I have to say anything?"

He frowned. "Their accent may be slow, but their minds aren't. People in Kiptohanock can count. They know your husband's been dead for three years. You don't want people thinking the worst."

"The worst?" She gestured at her belly. "You think this is the worst? Let me tell you about worst, little brother."

"I'm thinking of your reputation, Anna."

"By the time I was twenty-eight, I'd already suffered the worst day of my life. Holding the hand of my husband as he breathed his last breath." Her lips twisted. "People need to mind their own business."

"It's not that simple, Anna." He flexed his jaw. "And you know it."

Evy touched Anna's hand. "I don't think you're giving people enough credit. They will want to help."

Like Ryan? Except for God, she'd felt alone for a long time. She wouldn't have survived without His help. She believed in the deepest part of her being this baby was part of God's plan for her.

"I have to do this, Charlie," she whispered.

Her brother rose with a groan. "I guess I have no choice but to let you do this your way."

Evy helped her off the couch. "Don't forget how much we love you and want to be here for you, Anna."

She hugged the petite woman who'd become the closest thing to a sister she'd ever known. Saying a quick goodbye before her resolve weakened, Anna lumbered out the door. And nearly fell off the wide-planked porch in disbelief.

Ankles crossed and arms folded, Ryan leaned against her car.

She had a hard time regaining her breath and not only because she walked the distance between the living room and veranda. "What're you doing here?"

"You caught me by surprise before." Behind the frames, his eyes flickered. "I wanted to apologize for walking away. Congratulations, Anna. You'll be a wonderful mother."

Sudden warmth flooded her chest. He had no idea how much his words meant.

"You asked me to trust you, Anna. So I do." He ran his hand over his hair. "I don't understand this situation at all, but I promise to never stop being your friend."

Her throat constricted.

Pushing off from the car, he came forward to the bottom step. "Will you forgive me for being an idiot and give me another chance to be the friend you deserve?"

"I'd like that, Ryan." Tears stung her eyes. "Very much."

He gave her that crooked smile she remembered so well. Like a flash of lightning, momentarily sizzling her brain.

"I figured Charlie might need help unpacking your car." He motioned to the packed-to-the-roof baby blue Beetle. "Looks like the day you headed off to college. Remember?"

She remembered.

A tender moment on a long-ago August morning when he helped pack her stuff into this same car. When she'd hoped for something more than friendship. But now? If he only understood how little of that girl remained.

"I've rented a small house on Quayside Lane."

He shrugged. "Then I'll follow and help you unpack."

"That's not necessary."

"Or I won't believe you've really forgiven me." He cocked his head. "You don't want me lying awake all night on your conscience, do you, Anna Banana?"

Her lips quirked.

No fair playing on his affectionate childhood nickname for her. Maybe this once, it wouldn't hurt to let someone help carry the load. She glanced at the overloaded vehicle. Literally.

"If you want to."

He laughed. "Perhaps the most begrudging acceptance I've ever heard."

It wouldn't do to become too dependent on anyone. Not even her dearest friend. "What I meant to say was thank you, Ryan. I'd appreciate your help."

To show him her sincerity, she gave him a wide smile. But when she took hold of his hand to descend the steps, an unexpected tingle shot from his fingers to her elbow.

Ground level, she jerked free. Their gazes locked.

Something flamed in the blue-green depths of his eyes. "By the way, Anna, Merry Christmas."

"Is it?" she rasped.

He broke eye contact long enough to push his glasses farther along the bridge of his nose. "I think, for the first time in a long while, it might just be a very merry Christmas."

"Friends?" Something compelled her to add.

He scraped his hand over the beard stubble on his jaw. "Friends."

Anna owed him the truth. Not everyone in Kiptohanock would understand her decision to carry this child. Would Ryan?

She exhaled, sending a puff of breath into the brisk air. "The baby is Mateo's. Posthumously conceived. So a tiny part of the life we shared can live on."

"I meant what I said. I'm here for you." He swallowed. "For as long as you'll let me."

Good as his word, he wouldn't let her down. Ryan Savage had never let her down. And somehow in the deep places of her heart, she knew he wouldn't now.

He cleared his throat. "In fact, I've made some phone calls..."

She glanced at him.

"I'm going to be your own personal version of Santa. And I could use your help with an idea I have for Maria, Oscar and Zander."

"Which means what?"

"I'm going to make it my mission to make this the best Kiptohanock Christmas ever." He smiled, and her heart lurched. "For all of us."

Chapter Three

Dusk fell as Ryan hauled the last box up the rickety, wooden steps into the run-down trailer. He placed the box on the peeling kitchen countertop. No wonder Anna hadn't wanted her brother out here.

She raised her palm before he could speak. "It was cheap. It was furnished. It's temporary and not any of your business."

"You can't stay here, Anna. The steps are an accident waiting to happen."

She folded her arms. "I'll be fine."

"And that car you got as a high school graduation present is on its last legs. I can't believe you drove from Texas in that bucket of bolts."

"My car is fine."

"You and I both know that at the crack of dawn, your brother is going to pay you a visit. And then he's going to drag you out of here if he has to put you under house arrest—his house—to do it."

In her defiant brown eyes, for a second he glimpsed the take-no-sass girl raised in a houseful of boys. "He can try."

She wasn't the only one who could do stubborn. "I'm fixing the steps, Anna."

"I'll fix the steps myself."

He planted his hands on his hips. "Can you see your feet, Anna, much less crawl under the porch?"

She rocked back. Wrong thing to say to a pregnant woman.

"I didn't mean that the way—" But she sidestepped his outstretched hand.

Frustration bubbled at her mile-wide independent streak. "I can't in good conscience let you get hurt on those steps."

"Conscience's sake? Is that why you're here?" Her lips flattened. "What am I, Ryan, this year's Christmas project?"

He moved around the kitchen island toward her. "Absolutely not."

She pressed her spine against the speckled counter. "Knock yourself out then. Don't let me stop you."

"Anna, I just—"

"By all means do what you have to do so you can sleep at night." She inched past him, not an easy feat with the lack of square footage in the tiny galley kitchen.

As for the electric spark when he touched her hand on Charlie's porch? He clamped down on his jaw.

Friends. They were friends. He drilled it into his brain. Just friends.

Retrieving the toolbox from the trunk of his car, he did what he could in the fading light to make the hand railing more secure. The steps needed a total overhaul. But in the meantime...

Poking her head out the door, Anna flicked a switch inside the house. An exterior light blinked to feeble life.

He glanced up. "I'm done for the night."

"Thank you, Ryan. Don't let me keep you from..." She

fluttered her hand in the general direction of the mainland United States. "Wherever you go in the evenings."

"From my wife and kids, you mean?"

The strangest look crossed her face, so quickly he almost believed he imagined it. "I didn't realize you had a wife and children."

"I don't."

"Oh." She moistened her bottom lip with her tongue. "Good."

He cocked his head. "Good I don't have a wife and kids?"

"Yes—no..." She reddened. "I mean, good that I'm not keeping you from anything. Like supper." She cleared her throat. "I should pay you."

He frowned. "I don't want you to pay me."

Earning him a mulish look.

"On second thought, maybe you *are* keeping me from my supper." He chucked the hammer. It clattered into the metallic toolbox. "And since you have to eat, too, we might as well keep each other company."

She stiffened. "Why?"

He leaned against the railing, testing his weight against it. "You need to eat. I need to eat." He glanced at her basketball-size belly. "The baby needs for you to eat. And there's something else you can keep me from."

She rested her hand on top of her stomach. "What's that?"

"You can keep me from another Friday night of eating alone." He grinned at her. "Dinner will give us a chance to catch up."

"Long time no see?"

"Our Christmas reunion. A lot has happened since we last saw each other."

"No kidding." Her gaze fell to the wooden steps. "I'm

sorry about your dad, Ryan." She dropped her hand to her side. "Mateo was going through chemo and…"

"We lost touch. No problem. Dinner?"

Her lashes feathered her skin. "I never could say no to you."

Which wasn't how he remembered high school. Though more often than not, he hadn't given her a chance to say no. He'd been too scared to ask Anna to prom. He reckoned it best to be content being best friends.

He made sure she locked the door. Another item on his To-Do list. Wouldn't take much effort to break the lock on the wobbly doorknob. He'd feel better knowing Anna was safe at night out here alone. Ryan offered his arm as she descended the steps.

Instead, she gripped the bannister. "I got it. Thanks for making the railing sturdier."

He stationed himself at ground level in case she needed him. Not that Anna Pruitt had ever needed him. He'd been the one who foolishly hoped their friendship might blossom into something more. "How 'bout Tammy and Johnny's for burgers and fries?"

"Boot?" Her lips curved. "It's been a long time since I've heard me some Shore talk."

He rolled his tongue in his cheek. "Which simply means it's been too long since you've been graced by our unique Tidewater dialect."

She smiled as she crossed the oyster-shelled driveway to his car. "Dutch treat."

He opened the passenger door. "I'm not going to argue with you about dinner. It's my treat."

"That doesn't seem fair considering how much you've already helped me."

He kept the door between them. "I insist. For old times' sake."

"Old times." She backed into the seat. "Just let me stuff my beached whale self inside your car." She swung her legs inside last.

He tucked her red wool coat out of the way of the door. "You look beautiful."

It was true. She'd been a lovely girl. Pregnant, she glowed with a womanly luminescence.

She twisted at an awkward angle, reaching for the seat belt. "You're being kind."

"Let me." Leaning over her, he clicked the seat belt in position. Unconsciously, he inhaled her scent. A delicious blend of vanilla, cloves and cinnamon. Like Christmas. So like the Anna he remembered.

The air suddenly felt close. Rising abruptly, he banged his head on the roof. "Ow."

She took a ragged breath. "Are you okay?"

Grunting, he extricated himself and rubbed the top of his scalp. Rounding the hood, he slipped into the driver seat and concentrated on pulling out of her badly rutted driveway. He planned to give Charlie a call tonight. Between the two of them, they'd soon sort a few issues with her landlord.

She shifted in the seat. "How long was your father sick?"

"Mom called us home after his stroke four years ago. At rehab, Dad suffered another stroke two months later and died."

"Why did you stay?"

He negotiated a bend in the road. "The bills had piled up. The business was in danger of going under. With Mom working at the high school, someone had to keep the business afloat. We all helped with the garden center and farm."

She placed her palm atop her abdomen. "The Savage

siblings rallied." Her eyes flitted to his. "I've always loved how supportive y'all are to each other."

"Y'all." His lips twitched. "Glad to see you can take the girl out of the South, but you can't take the South out of the girl." He bypassed the turnoff for Kiptohanock.

She swatted his arm. Like old times.

He grinned. "Luke does the actual horticultural work. Justine gave up her art gallery to run the garden center. But Ethan had to finish his enlistment first. Once Tess completed her degree, she came home, too."

"My mother tells me you gave up your career."

He swallowed, touched that she'd gone to the trouble of keeping track of him over the years. "Once a science geek, always a science geek."

"You were never a geek, Mr. Track Star. In fact, you were always too cool for school." She patted the dashboard. "You're still rocking the laid-back vibe." A smile played across her lips.

He arched his eyebrow. "'Cause it doesn't get cooler than a Saab?"

She laughed and pointed at the radio. "Harry Connick or Sinatra?"

Ryan smiled. "Probably their holiday CDs. As I recall, you start celebrating in October."

"Not anymore." She sighed. "Since Mateo died, Christmas is something to just get through."

Pulling off the highway, he steered into the crowded roadside hangout. It pained him to hear her talk like that. "You have so much to look forward to. And next year will be the baby's first Christmas."

Her expression closed. "Did you see Oscar's face when he mentioned Christmas?"

Ryan took the hint. Talk of the future made Anna uneasy. "Until Zander shot him down like an eight-year-old Grinch."

"When I think back to the wonderful childhood memories I have, it hurts my heart to imagine what Christmas has been like for those kids."

He turned off the engine. "After we eat, I could use your help on making this Christmas a happy one for them. But we'll have to hurry to implement Phase One of Operation Christmas."

Operation Christmas?

Perhaps Ryan was on to something. She could think of no one she'd rather see happy than those children. Spending time with the handsome teacher would be a plus.

Inside, he wouldn't allow her to pay for her meal. "Pick a seat." He motioned. "I'll wait for the food."

Not drifting far, she'd no sooner chosen a seat than two children ran over to him. Max and Izzie, two of his fifth graders.

"Are you coming tonight, Mr. Savage?"

"You gotta come, Mr. Savage."

He grinned at them. "Since you've known me, have I ever missed the flotilla parade?"

Was that tonight? Anna would eat fast so as not to keep him from other commitments. The children rejoined a group of adults and younger children. Caroline and Amelia Duer. Their mother and Ryan's father had been siblings. The sisters and Ryan were first cousins.

She was less pleased by the other women, who, one by one, sidled over to the bachelor teacher. With his lanky build and the swimming-pool eyes behind the frames, he was not merely popular with children.

No surprise, he remained a chick magnet. There was

something irresistible about a man so not interested in becoming attached.

On second thought, he never said he wasn't attached. She squirmed on the hard plastic seat. Only that he wasn't married.

A line of women floated past Ryan at the drink dispensary. If he wasn't already attached, it wasn't from lack of trying on the part of the Shore's female residents.

Carrying the tray, he sank into the seat opposite Anna. "Sorry it took so long."

She pursed her lips. "The plight of a handsome heartthrob."

He set the tray down. "What?"

Whether he was truly unattached or not really didn't fall into the "just friends" category. But the itch to know wouldn't leave her.

She reached for her milkshake. Babies needed dairy, right? "I find it hard to believe you haven't been taken off the market by a girlfriend." She bit into a french fry.

His blue eyes dropped to half-mast. "Actually, I was engaged when Dad got sick."

The fry lodged in her throat. She choked. He thrust his water cup at her.

She took a quick gulp. A fiancée? Why had no one mentioned that detail over the years?

"Thanks." She pushed away the fries, her appetite gone. "*Was* engaged?"

"I thought I was in love." He looked away. "I believed she was in love with me. I was wrong on both counts."

Someone hurt him. Badly. "What happened?"

His jaw tightened. "Karen was a research analyst at the same pharmaceutical company. When Dad got sick, I came home." He combed his hand through the short hair on the nape of his neck. "Karen broke things off. She couldn't envision herself living in this, and I quote, 'beach-side backwater.'"

Anna placed her hand over his on the table. "And after you sacrificed so much, you lost her, too."

"I'm no hero, Anna." He shook his head. "I was bitter for a long time. But stripped of everything I'd pursued so relentlessly, I rediscovered God. Dad's death hit us hard. I needed to be there for the family so I took the only job for which I was remotely qualified. Teaching on a then-provisional license."

She suspected he was adept at hiding his pain. "I'm sorry you had to give up your dream."

He shrugged. "With an educator for a mother, maybe a teaching gene has always been part of my DNA."

"Spoken like the scientist you are." His hand felt warm and strong against hers. "Based on that theory, I should either be a nurse or a deputy sheriff."

At the same moment, they both seemed to realize they were still touching. He withdrew his hand, and she dropped hers into her lap.

He handed her a wrapped burger. "You still faint at the sight of blood, Anna Banana?" The corners of his mouth curved. "Leastways, Charlie followed in your dad's foot-steps."

"Like you followed in your mom's."

He toyed with the burger. "Only till Christmas."

Anna's stomach knotted. "I don't understand."

He crossed his arms. "This isn't for public consumption. The family and Principal Carden know, but no one else."

She swallowed. "Know what?"

"I'm leaving for my old pharmaceutical job in North Carolina after Christmas."

"What about your family?" Her voice hitched. "What

about your class? Our after-school group?" *What about me?* she wanted to ask but didn't.

"Mom and the rest of the family are finally ready to move on with their lives. Mr. Carden has already found a teacher for my class." He made a wry grimace. "Turns out I'm easily replaced."

"I don't think your fifth graders, Maria, Oscar or Zander would agree."

"They'll like the guy who's taking my place. He has more experience working with at-risk kids, too."

But no matter how great the new teacher proved to be, he'd never be Ryan.

"Sounds like you've thought of everything."

He nodded. "It's a done deal. It will be good to get back to the lab where I belong."

Disappointment swelled within Anna.

His face became animated as he told her about the exciting research team he'd be joining. "The drug we're developing has the potential to change the lives of thousands of people."

She couldn't believe he was leaving just when she'd come back. Their lives had always been at cross-purposes. She should be happy for him. It was obviously what he'd worked so hard to achieve.

"I'm happy for you, Ryan." Maybe saying it would make it so. But she didn't feel any better. She'd probably have to say it a dozen more times to make it real.

He ran his hand over his head, a sign of uncertainty with him. "Now that the business is stable, there's nothing else to keep me here." An expression she couldn't decipher crisscrossed his face. "Is there?"

She laced her fingers together in her lap. "I guess some things don't change. Like the difference between you and me."

He tilted his head. "What difference?"

"When I left for college, I didn't dream I'd be gone fourteen years." She rested her hand on her abdomen. "I never planned or wanted to live anywhere else."

He met her gaze head-on. "Whereas I always wanted to leave."

"I remember." Her voice softened. "And you can't wait to leave again."

"How much of the world did you see before Mateo—?" He scrubbed his hand over his beard stubble. "Sorry."

"It's okay to talk about Mateo, Ryan. I won't fall apart. Restationed every few years, we managed to see a lot of the United States." She placed her palms flat on either side of the tray. "But most of all, Mateo wanted to start a family."

Ryan pushed the tray aside. "What did you want?"

"I wanted to be a mother, too, only—"

Only her selfishness had cost her husband the chance to know his child.

"I believed Mateo and I had plenty of time…" She worked to control the trembling of her chin. "Turns out I was wrong."

"Then we'll have to make the most of the time we have."

She glanced at him. "What do you mean?"

"Operation Christmas. The number listed in the file for Zander has been disconnected." Ryan propped his elbows on the table. "But I was able to reach Oscar's mom and got permission to take him to the Flotilla of Lights tonight in the harbor. Wanna give the kid a little taste of Christmas?"

"But—"

"I didn't forget about Maria. Her folks already plan to attend."

It had been so long since she attended a Kiptohanock Christmas boat parade.

"Unless…" He deflated. "You're tired. I can take you home first. Or if you think it's a bad idea—"

"Are you kidding?" She lifted her chin. "I wouldn't miss seeing Oscar's face for the world."

He smiled that slow, lopsided smile of his. Setting off an unfamiliar seismic reaction in her heart.

This was about the children, she reminded herself. Sternly. "Operation Christmas, Phase One, right?"

"Exactly." He rubbed his palms together. "This is going to be fun. Get ready for the Christmas of your life."

And she had the feeling that somehow it would be— maybe in more ways than she could yet imagine.

Chapter Four

Thirty minutes later, Ryan parked outside the seedy, run-down motel. Only the neon sign relieved the darkness of the night.

Anna's frown reflected his own misgivings. "Oscar lives here?"

"No. At least, I don't think so." Ryan got out of the car. "But this is where his mother told me to pick him up."

Anna unbuckled her seat belt.

He frowned. "I don't want you going into a place like this, but I also don't want to leave you here while I go inside."

Anna got out of the car. "I'm not worried." She smiled. "I feel safe with you."

She'd always made him feel safe, too. Safe to be himself.

An inebriated couple lurched out of the entrance. Tensing, Ryan placed himself between Anna and them. But the pair headed deeper into the shadows of the parking lot, and Ryan slipped Anna inside the motel lobby.

Only a small lamp on the front desk relieved the gloominess. The carpet reeked of cigarette smoke and something else he preferred not to identify. Behind the desk, a young girl glared.

At a scuttling sound low to the floor, Anna shrank into him. Her grip on his arm became a stranglehold.

"Maybe it's a good thing there's not more lighting."

Anna grimaced. "Because if we could see what was moving, we'd be really scared?"

The girl at the desk curled her stud-pierced lip. "Can I help you?"

She wasn't as young as he'd first believed. Early twenties. His youngest sister Tessa's age. But it was her eyes that snared his attention. Blue chips of hopelessness. Her ash-blond hair was his first clue she might be Oscar's mother.

The woman's hands gripped the edge of the counter. "You want the hourly rate?"

"No." He stiffened. "We're not—"

"Are you Oscar's mother?" Anna stepped around him. "Mrs. Ericson?"

The woman's features hardened. "Never been married. It's Miz Ericson." Her eyes narrowed. "Though nobody's ever called me that, either."

She didn't offer her given name, but Anna smiled. "I'm Anna Reyes. One of Oscar's teachers in the after-school program."

He shouldn't have brought Anna here. She didn't belong in a place like this. Ryan's gaze flickered. Nobody belonged in a place like this.

The young woman assessed him with laser sharpness. "You the teacher who called here?"

He cleared his throat. "I called the only number listed in Oscar's file."

"Yeah, well…" The young woman gave an elaborate shrug. Her shirt rose, revealing a navel ring.

"We hoped we might take Oscar to see the boat parade tonight," Anna broke in. "If that's okay with you?"

"I told you to come, didn't I?"

At one time the young woman might've been pretty. But life had not been kind to her. And he was overcome with doubt.

What had he been thinking? Taking a kid to a Christmas parade was just a bandage on a larger problem. The issues facing this family were complex. He was in over his head.

Making an excuse was on the tip of his tongue. But the memory of Oscar's pinched face wouldn't leave him. And instead of exiting, Ryan found himself going in deeper. "We might also stop by McDonald's afterward if you don't mind, Ms. Ericson."

In her eyes, a desperate gratitude battled with an overwhelming shame. "It's Brittany. And that would be nice of you." She blinked and looked away. "Oscar hasn't had a Happy Meal in a long time." She leaned behind the front desk. "Oscar? Wake up, son."

Ryan and Anna exchanged glances. Oscar was sleeping behind the front desk on the filthy floor?

"Your teachers are here, Oscar. Wake up. Remember, I told you they were coming?"

His sleep-rumpled blond head emerged. A floppy-eared stuffed elephant that had seen better days was carefully tucked in the crook of his elbow. His mother drew him out from behind the counter.

She smoothed the cowlick on his head. "You're gonna love the pretty lights." Bending to his height, she fished a coin out of her jeans pocket and thrust a quarter at her son. "Take this. In case you need it. Don't be no trouble for your teachers."

Oscar hugged Anna's knees so hard she staggered. "I'm so happy to see you, Miz Reyes." Anna hugged him back.

His mother straightened. Red peppered her cheeks. "No need to hurry him home." Her mouth thinned on the last word. "It gets busy around here when darkness falls."

An awkward silence descended. That was their cue to leave.

"Bye, Mama." Oscar waved.

Holding the door, Ryan cast one final glance over his shoulder. Just in time to see Brittany's hard, brittle shell crack for a moment as a single tear ran down her cheek.

On the way to the holiday flotilla, Anna found herself singing alongside Bing Crosby's rendition of "It's Beginning to Look a Lot Like Christmas" on the radio.

From the back seat booster Ryan had borrowed, Oscar hummed along, not really knowing the words. "This is gonna be the funnest night ever, Mister Sabbage."

Ryan's eyes cut to the rearview mirror. "Yes, it is, Oscar. The best."

As they drove into town, Kiptohanock did indeed look a lot like Christmas. Sitting high in the seat, Oscar made little sounds of happiness at the sight of the decorated homes. Anna glanced over at Ryan.

He was a special man to have taken on something like this to bring Christmas joy to a needy kid like Oscar. Her respect for her old friend grew.

Ryan pulled into an empty space in the cafe parking lot. "Let me unbuckle Oscar first, then I'll come around for you."

"Not necessary, Ryan."

He gave her a teacher look over the rim of his glasses. "How about letting a guy be a gentleman, Anna Banana?"

Childish laughter erupted from the back seat. "She's not a banana, Mister Sabbage."

"Thanks for setting me straight, Oscar." His mouth twitched. "What about it, Miz Reyes?"

"Fine." She held up her palm. "Whatever you say, Mister Sabbage."

He flashed her a quick grin—his hunky demeanor like a sucker punch to her gut. He and Oscar helped her unfold from the passenger side.

"Will your family be here tonight, Ryan?"

Ryan and Oscar each took one of her hands and tugged. "Probably not. Christmas Open House at the garden center tomorrow."

She found her footing as Ryan and Oscar high-fived. "Teamwork!" Ryan smiled at her. "Let's go have fun."

Anna took Oscar's hand as they crossed the parking lot to join the throng gathering around the seawall. The lanterns on the square pulsed with a warm glow. Holiday music blared from the loudspeakers at the Coast Guard station.

Many townsfolk stopped to welcome Anna home. Though she could see the questions on people's faces at her rounded abdomen, their welcome was nonetheless genuine. And everyone proved kind to Oscar, as well.

Friends of her parents like Dixie, a waitress at the cafe, and her husband, Bernard. The Reverend Parks and Agnes. When their daughter, Darcy, came up and hugged her, she and Anna both squealed like the two teenage girls they'd been a long time ago.

"Lunch. Soon," Anna promised as Oscar pulled her closer to the marina, where fishing vessels and pleasure boats were decked out in multicolored lights.

Chums of her absentee brothers said their hellos. Many of them were married and had children of their own now. Children, like Oscar, who waited with barely concealed anticipation for the arrival of Father Kiptohanock. Spotting her teachers, Maria dragged her family over to meet them.

Maria's mother toted a baby on her hip. A toddler perched on her father's shoulders. The Guzmans spoke very little English, but Maria and Oscar chatted easily. It was the most animated she'd seen Maria yet.

Standing next to her brother, Sawyer Kole, Evy waved from the edge of the town dock. On duty, Charlie was probably somewhere overseeing security.

"Would you like to join Evy?" Ryan's breath made puffs of air.

"Let's stay here so Maria and Oscar can enjoy the parade together." She scanned the nearby church, open for potential emergencies. At least that's what she hoped. "These days it's best to never get too far from a bathroom."

He laughed, the sound rumbling out of his chest.

She was reminded of how close he'd been in the car when he fastened her seat belt. And how he smelled of Old Spice and spearmint gum.

Her pulse did an unauthorized staccato step. "I'll stay here with the kids and the Guzmans. But you can go." A little distance might prove wise.

"I'm right where I want to be." He settled in beside her.

Shoulder to shoulder at the seawall, she forced herself not to inhale too deeply. It wasn't as if she were trying to capture his scent again in her nostrils. That would be too ridiculous. And pathetic. Despite the chilly temperature, her cheeks burned with an awareness of him.

Hands stuffed in the pockets of his coat, he smiled at her. For an instant, something blazed in his eyes. But before she could identify the emotion, he turned toward the water. "Think we'll have a white Christmas?"

She gulped past the boat-size boulder lodged in her throat. "Has there ever been a white Christmas in Kiptohanock?"

Taking his hands out of his pockets, he leaned his elbows on top of the wall. "My gram used to tell us about one white Christmas when she was a girl."

"Doesn't seem fair, does it?" She shrugged. "The cold temperatures without the reward of snow."

"Make it your Christmas wish, Anna." The corner of his mouth lifted, zinging straight to her heart. "And tell it to Father Kiptohanock." His gaze flicked toward the harbor. "It's starting."

Oscar and Maria strained forward as far as the seawall allowed. Vessels decorated like parade floats chugged past the judges on the dock. Charter boats with cutout cardboard Christmas trees glowed red and green.

Max and his dad, Chief Braeden Scott, waved to the crowd from one of the sailboats. A Star of Bethlehem on top of the mast and a blue string of lights festooned their entry.

Adorned with neon cats and dogs, the Santa Paws boat encouraged people to adopt a pet. Flags aflutter, the Coasties had embellished a rapid response boat in red, white and blue. Izzie Clark waved in a queenlike fashion from onboard the sea turtle hospital float.

Ryan chuckled. "Izzie and Max. Always a competition with those two. Yet the best of friends."

She elbowed him. "Remind you of anyone?"

Ryan elbowed her back. "And here we are, the two of us, teaching the bright young minds of Kiptohanock. Full circle, huh?"

Her smile faded. *Only temporarily.* Ryan was leaving after Christmas.

Oscar tugged her arm. "Look, Miz Reyes."

Decked out like a pirate ship, the high school float loaded with students maneuvered past the wharf. A tall, gangly boy lifted his imitation hook and whooped. A teenage girl with flowing dark hair and an eye patch brandished a fake sword. On the shoreline, a ruggedly handsome man and a blonde pregnant woman broke into cheers.

"Is that—?" Anna started to point but thought better of it.

Ryan clapped furiously as the students hammed it up for the judges. "Yes, it is," he whispered. "One of the Colliers."

She tried not to let her jaw drop. "Not the one who…?"

He shook his head. "That one's still in jail. This is his older brother, Canyon. A respected agriculture pilot now. Lives in the family homeplace. The swashbuckling girl pirate is his. Canyon married the widowed mother of Captain Hook. She owns the florist shop."

Anna smiled. "From the looks of things, it's his, hers and theirs."

Ryan folded his arms across his chest. "They found their happily-ever-after after much heartache. Kristina lost her first husband in Afghanistan."

Anna's heart stirred with sympathy for the woman who appeared to be in her first trimester. "I had friends on the base who lost their husbands that way, too. Sudden and horrific."

"What you endured was as horrific as losing a husband to combat, Anna." Ryan closed his eyes momentarily. "Perhaps worse."

"Either way." She sighed. "Goodbyes are never easy."

"No." He stared out over the color-dappled water. "They're not."

Did he pine for the woman who'd broken their engagement? The woman must've been an idiot to bail on a man like Ryan. Great guys weren't a dime a dozen. She'd found one in Mateo. Ryan, her dear friend, was no less a prize for some woman to claim.

She inhaled sharply. Some woman, not her.

"Are you okay?" He made a move to touch her but let his hand fall to his side. "Do you need to sit down?"

"I'm fine. Got to get my teacher legs back. Anyway, I'm

glad to see Canyon Collier and his lady got their happy ending." She placed her hand on her abdomen, rubbing small circles on her belly.

"You were born to be a mother, Anna. You'll be the best."

"I hope so." She patted his arm. "By the way, I like the scruffy look on you."

He snorted. "Thank you, I think."

"I mean it." She nudged him with her shoulder. "You rock the intellectual vibe."

He rolled his eyes. "You mean the geeky vibe."

"I mean the too cool for school, good-looking—"

"You think I'm good-looking?"

She blushed.

"Thank you, Anna."

And they shared a look from which she couldn't turn away. Her pulse pounded.

Ryan gestured to the end of the pier, where the judges handed out the award for Best Powerboat to the Coasties. "Nobody does Christmas better than Kiptohanock."

She gave him a sideways look. "And yet you're leaving."

He could hardly believe he was standing on the waterfront with Anna after all these years. How many times had he wished…? He shook himself. Best not to get too attached. She was right. He was leaving.

The excitement in the crowd ratcheted as the judges awarded the remaining prizes. Braeden Scott won best in the sailboat division. Ten-year-old Max smirked at his glowering archrival, Izzie.

But the sea turtle float scored People's Choice. The little redheaded girl smirked right back at Max. Santa Paws garnered Best in Show. The high school captured the Best Costume and Best Crew Spirit award.

And finally what everyone had been waiting for. With electric reindeer mounted on the bow, one last vessel negotiated the waters between the anchored parade participants. Excited, Maria and Oscar bobbed like baited hooks in the water. Mrs. Guzman and Anna exchanged smiles.

Father Kiptohanock threw a mooring line to a Coastie, who tied the boat to the dock cleats. Applause ensued. Father Kiptohanock—like an old-time waterman but in a faux fur-trimmed red slicker and Wellingtons—stepped onto the wharf.

Anna's mouth fell open. "Is that Seth Duer?"

"Not so loud." Ryan laid his finger on his lips. "It's Seth's turn this year. Margaret Davenport made sure he didn't weasel out of it."

"Margaret's still orchestrating Kiptohanock life?"

The sixty-something lady was as well-known and Shore-famous as the Sandpiper's Long John doughnuts. In her case, though, it was for her meddling, autocratic ways and sharp tongue.

He did a half-hearted fist pump. "Long live the Queen."

Released from parental restraints, Maria, Oscar and the other children swarmed Seth Duer—aka Father Kiptohanock—for the anticipated candy. And Ryan's heart swelled when Oscar shared his candy with Maria's little brother. Oscar was a good kid. A kid in need of a helping hand.

Anna giggled. "Is it my imagination, or does Father Kiptohanock resemble a Yuletide Gorton's Fisherman?"

"Minus the beard." Ryan grinned. "But I think the bushy mustache counts."

She laughed so hard she braced against the seawall for support. "Only in Kiptohanock."

He got the feeling it was the first time in a long while that she'd laughed—really laughed.

Then he spotted Margaret Davenport plowing her way

through the onlookers. At the determined gleam in her eyes, he wondered who she had in her sights. And with dismay, realized it was none other than Anna.

He broadened his chest. If she'd come to criticize Anna, she'd have to go through him first. Nobody was dissing Anna on his watch.

Anna's smile faded as she glanced at his face. "What's—?"

"I'm so glad I caught the two of you." Margaret's gaze pinged from Ryan to Anna. "Nice to see you home again, Anna."

Anna's hand flew protectively over her stomach.

Margaret focused on Ryan. "Your brother promised me he'd have those animals for the Living Nativity by Christmas week."

"If Luke said he'd have them, then—"

"Fine." She fluttered an imperious hand. "Actually, I came over to talk with Anna."

He widened his stance. "I don't think—"

"I believe congratulations are in order, Anna." Margaret's face softened. "I'm sorry your husband will not be here to share in your joy."

He probed the older woman's expression for signs of derision but found none. Only a compassion he'd not expected in the usually acerbic grande dame of Kiptohanock.

"Forgive me for asking this of you, Anna." Margaret's voice hitched. "I was never blessed with children myself." She fussed with the buttons on her coat. "The wonders of modern science. Not like when I was your age…"

He gaped at Margaret.

Somehow the grapevine of Kiptohanock knew the whole story about Anna's baby. It had to be Evy. The young librarian and the town matriarch had become inexplicably close friends since Evy first came to town.

Margaret's eyes became misty. "I always believed it would be so wonderful to carry a child at Christmas."

Anna's eyes were huge, like a fish caught in a spotlight.

Margaret fidgeted. "Would you consider playing the mother of Jesus in the Living Nativity…?" Her voice trailed away.

He'd never seen Margaret so…un-Margaretlike.

Eyes lowered to the ground, Margaret backpedaled. "Never mind, dear. I shouldn't have—" Her voice choked. "It's not as though this is your home anymore or—"

"Of course I'll do it."

Margaret halted, midstep.

"Kiptohanock will be my home from now on." Anna rested her hand atop her belly. "I'd love to play Mary in the nativity, Margaret."

He frowned. "Anna…"

She raised her gaze. "Just tell me when and where."

Margaret blinked twice before recovering her usual aplomb. "There will be costume fittings. And the one night performance during Christmas week in the gazebo on the square." She tapped her finger on her chin. "I still need to find a Joseph, of course."

As if one entity, Anna and Margaret cut their eyes at him. He shuffled his feet. But surrounded and outnumbered, nothing less than unconditional surrender would suffice.

Besides, how could he resist the opportunity to play Anna's husband, even if it was just pretend?

"Okay. My arm's twisted. I'm in."

Margaret clasped her hands together. "I can't wait to tell the other ladies." She moved away. "I'll send you both the details. This is going to be the best Kiptohanock Christmas ever."

He groaned. "Where have I heard that before?"

Anna poked him in his biceps. "Your famous last words, I believe. And your arm doesn't look too twisted to me." She laughed. "Where's your Christmas spirit, Ryan Savage? It'll be fun."

He grunted. "This is Margaret we're talking about."

She stared after the older woman's retreating figure. "She's changed. The town has, too." She heaved a sigh. "Or maybe it's me that changed."

He crinkled his eyes. "The more things change, the more they remain the same. I hate to end the fun, but we better get going if we're going to buy Oscar a Happy Meal."

Anna's face shadowed. "I don't want to take him back to the motel."

He sighed. "Me, either, but she's his mother."

"Something needs to be done about his situation."

Ryan's life had suddenly gotten so much more complicated. He was supposed to be wrapping up his teaching career, not getting more involved.

"Does his mother work there every night? Is that why he can't get a good night's rest?"

He scrubbed his jaw. "I should make a home visit when she's not at work. See what the school could do to connect them to one of the county programs."

"You always know the right thing to do."

He made a face. "That's me. Mr. Dependability. Mr. Reliable. Mr. Boring." He called to Oscar. Maria's father and mother hugged Oscar goodbye and waved them off.

Strolling toward the parking lot, Anna took hold of Oscar's hand. "You're not boring, Ryan. You're nice."

"Nice…" Ryan clutched his heart. "Kill me now and be done with it, Anna Banana."

Oscar ran over to the car.

"Nice is nothing to be ashamed of." She tucked her

hands into her coat pockets. "And that's not how I see you. You're also—" Her cheeks reddened.

Good-looking? That's what she'd said earlier. And feeling as carefree as he'd felt in years, he opened the door for Oscar.

Oscar jumped inside. "It's beginning to look like Christmas, Mister Sabbage."

An unfamiliar excitement began to build inside Ryan. Yes, it certainly was.

Chapter Five

The next morning Anna arrived at the trailer from a long overdue grocery trip to find Ryan fixing the steps of her porch. Laying aside the nail gun, he rose as she parked next to his car.

When she reached for a grocery bag, he hurried over. "Let me help, Anna."

"I'm pregnant, Ryan, not an invalid."

Grabbing two bags, he ignored her. Resigning herself to his helpfulness, she escorted him to the door.

He waited while she fumbled inside her purse for the key. "You were out early for a Saturday morning."

Inserting the key, she gave it a turn, but the doorknob twisted in her hand.

He handed her the lightest of the sacks. "Let me try."

Jiggling the key, he lifted up on the knob and shoved the door with his shoulder. "Voilà!" He motioned as the door swept open.

She stepped over the threshold. "You are amazing."

He carried the bags to the kitchen. "That's what the kids tell me."

She gave him a sideways glance. "Their moms, too."

He pushed at his glasses with his forefinger. "What?"

"Never mind." She unpacked the bread. "I didn't expect to see you this morning."

He unloaded another bag, handing her the items. "I told you I'd fix the steps."

She put away the cereal. "Thank you."

He placed the milk jug inside the harvest gold refrigerator. "The lock is next on my list."

"Ryan, I appreciate your concern, but—"

"Where do you want the coffee?"

She gave him her best teacher glare. He grinned, unfazed.

Hand propped, she jutted her hip. "No matter what I say, you're going to do the repairs anyway, aren't you?"

Ryan shrugged. "I'm enjoying myself."

"Enjoying yourself?" She shivered. "It's freezing out there."

"I like to keep busy."

"Surely you can think of something more fun to do with your free time." She brushed the pad of her thumb across his cheek.

His expression changed. Why had she touched him? Disconcerted, she dropped her hand.

"I enjoy doing things for you, Anna. Let somebody take care of you for once."

She busied herself with a sudden interest in the nutritional data on a box of rice. "Christmas was always one of your busiest seasons at the garden center. Aren't you needed there?"

"Despite the pride you take in being independent, helping around this place is a win-win for me." His eyes sharpened. "I get to spend more time with you."

Her mouth went dry. "Until you leave for your new job."

Ryan's gaze dropped to the floor. "Yes. Until then."

She took a steadying breath. "Aren't you helping with the open house?"

"My shift starts late afternoon." He refolded the empty brown paper bags. "Luke's got the Christmas tree stand under control. Trust me, Justine doesn't want me near the wreath-making. Ethan and Tess have a system for the sleigh rides and petting farm."

Anna leaned against the countertop. "I always thought it was so cool you lived on a farm."

He rolled his eyes. "Dad liked to start the weekend mornings early. Get as much free labor out of us kids as he could."

She crossed her arms over her belly. "Your dad was a wonderful man. You remind me of him."

A gentle smile teased Ryan's lips. "He was a great dad. Mom misses him a lot. We all do."

"Which is why each of you gave up your own lives to help preserve his legacy. And now you're helping Oscar, too."

"I'm not the hero you make me out to be." Ryan cocked his head. "Luke always loved the farm the most. But for me, Ethan, Justine and Tess, being here won't be forever."

Forever. Once, Anna believed she'd found her forever with Mateo. She laid her hand on top of her ever-expanding abdomen. But forever was turning out far different than she'd imagined. What did forever look like to Ryan?

She returned to putting away the last of the canned goods. Forever to Ryan probably looked like microscopes and test tubes.

"Oh, before I forget to tell you... I talked to your brother."

She raised her eyebrow. "Which one?"

"Charlie had a chat with your absentee landlord. I'm

keeping receipts on the repairs, and the cost will be deducted from your rent this month."

She'd been shocked to discover the trailer matched none of the online photos from the rental agency. "So I need to write you a reimbursement check."

"That's not what I meant."

She shut the cabinet door with a bang. "What did you mean then?"

"Charlie and I have your back, Anna." He made a palms-up gesture. "Let us help. Don't be so stubborn."

Her budget did need some breathing room. She hadn't bought any baby equipment yet. And baby stuff, especially on a single mother's salary, would be expensive.

"I appreciate everything you're doing, Ryan." She exhaled in a slow trickle of breath. "I really mean it."

And like the humble guy he'd always been, he deflected her praise. "That's what friends are for, right?"

Friends. Right. Her jaw tightened.

His eyes crinkled. "Back to Operation Christmas."

She pursed her lips. "Phase Two for the kids?"

"Actually, I was thinking of you."

Her heart thudded. "Me?"

Ryan ran his hand over the top of his head. "How about a field trip, Teach?"

She resisted the urge to smooth down the mess he'd made of his hair. "What kind of field trip?"

"A trip to the farm. What would Christmas be without a Savage Farm tree?"

"What indeed?" She did a slow twirl. "Am I dressed farm girl appropriate?"

He scanned her winter-white maternity sweater and the not-so-skinny black maternity jeans tucked into low-heeled boots. "You'll do." He smiled.

Anna wondered what his former fiancée, Karen, looked

like. Probably model thin and gorgeous. And then berated herself for being stupid. Though, she couldn't help but notice that Ryan made a point to never allow his attention to stray to her stomach.

She must look so huge and clumsy and unattractive to him. She'd always taken pride in her slim figure.

When he pulled the car off the main road and onto the long, gravel drive leading to the farm, for the first time she truly felt she'd come home. With her mom working hospital shifts and her dad's law enforcement hours, the farm had been a favorite hangout of hers as a teenager.

Greenhouses sat near the road. Fallow fields lay on either side of the rustic-looking garden center.

"Looks like Justine's busy." Ryan nudged his chin toward the nursery where cars filled the parking lot.

Her arms full of potted plants, Justine, a perky blonde, lifted her head at the sound of the approaching vehicle.

"Can we stop to say hello?"

Like a true brother, he gave an exaggerated sigh for Anna's benefit. "If we must."

Justine deposited the plants into the trunk of a green Subaru. "Anna Banana, welcome home." Her outstretched arms engulfed Anna, tummy and all.

"I see the news of my arrival has spread." Anna made a face. "As has my figure."

Justine stepped back. "You are as gorgeous as ever."

Anna sighed. "There's certainly more of me to admire these days."

"Congratulations, Anna." Justine's blue eyes sparkled. "I'm so happy for you."

Anna took her first deep breath of her Eastern Shore home. Here on the farm, she inhaled the pungent aroma of rich, loamy soil. From inside the store, a tantalizing whiff of cinnamon-spiced wassail laced the air. And a hint of pine floated from the surrounding forest.

Everything was as she remembered. Everything as it should be.

She spotted the potted plants in the trunk of the Subaru. "As I recall, poinsettias are your biggest seller this time of year."

Justine nodded. "Wreaths, too. Need one?"

She drew Anna over to a white lattice frame latched onto the side of the storefront from which hung a dozen fresh wreaths of pine, cedar and magnolia.

Anna smirked at Ryan. "This is a conspiracy, isn't it?"

He squared his broad shoulders. "Farmers and salesmen. It's what Savages do."

Justine elbowed his ribs. "That would be sales*persons*."

"Watch it, little sister." He poked her back. She scuttled out of reach.

Anna laughed. "Before the sibling rivalry escalates further, let me take the small one with the holly berries and red ribbon."

He winked at his sister. "Ka-ching…"

Justine smiled. "Works every time."

Anna whipped out her wallet before Ryan could object. "How much?"

Justine darted a glance at her brother. "There's a friends and family discount."

He took the wreath off the hook. "Exactly."

Justine took the money from Anna and headed into the storefront as the pregnant blonde woman from the flotilla last night emerged.

"Must be something in the water around here, huh?" She held out her hand. "I'm Kristina Collier. I don't believe we've met. Are you a new 'come here like me?"

Anna shook her hand. "More like a new 'come back here."

Ryan deposited the wreath in the car. "Anna is Charlie Pruitt's sister."

Kristina smiled. "Home for the holidays?"

"Not just for the holidays." Anna gave Ryan a pointed look. "I can't think of a better place to raise a family and build a life than here in Kiptohanock."

Ryan frowned. "There's more to life than sea air and sand."

Anna raised her chin. "Not if it's home."

Kristina nodded. "Home is where the heart is."

Ryan's eyes locked onto Anna's. "And Kiptohanock is where your heart is?"

Breathless at the intensity of his gaze, the rest of the world faded for Anna. "The heart wants what the heart wants."

A pulse ticked in his jaw. His mouth opened as if to answer, but Justine returned and handed Anna a steaming cup of wassail. "Would you help Kristina's husband load the rest of the poinsettias from the greenhouse, Ryan?"

"Sure." He pushed up the sleeves of his gray Duke University sweatshirt. "Duty calls." And he disappeared around the corner of the garden center to lend a hand.

Which was exactly how she remembered the Savage family. All for one and one for all. And despite Ryan's words to the contrary, his work on the farm was far more than duty.

She took a sip of the wassail. "You own the florist shop, Kristina?"

Canyon Collier, the handsome crop duster pilot, appeared with more plants cradled in his arms.

"A dream come true." Kristina's cornflower blue eyes

drifted to her husband. "Among many dreams come true recently."

Setting aside the plants, her husband laid his hand on his wife's just-beginning-to-show belly. Their palpable happiness filled Anna with an unsettling yearning for something she believed she'd forever laid to rest, choosing to focus her dreams on the baby.

But seeing them, a different sort of forever rose to the forefront of her mind. Involving beach, sand and fifth-grade teachers? She took a quick, scalding swallow and sputtered.

His arms full of plants, Ryan staggered into the car lot, interrupting the dangerous direction her thoughts had taken. "You okay?"

She flushed. No, she wasn't okay. Her grip tightened on the cup. "That's a lot of poinsettias."

Canyon and Justine deposited the rest of the flame-leafed pots into the hatch of the Collier vehicle.

Kristina angled around after her husband closed the hatch. "I'm on the church altar guild. We're decorating the sanctuary after lunch."

"That's everything." Justine gave Kristina a receipt. "Thanks for your business."

Kristina headed for the passenger side. "I'll need more greenery by Monday. I have orders for seasonal floral arrangements."

When the Colliers drove off, another customer approached, juggling pots of paper whites. Justine started forward to help. "Maybe we could get the old high school gang together again after Christmas."

Anna cut her eyes at Ryan. "Not sure that will work for everyone's schedule."

Ryan arched his eyebrow. "Before might be better."

Anna didn't smile. "Speak for yourself."

Justine waved goodbye as she moved away to help the overloaded customer.

Ryan rubbed his hands together. "How about getting you a Christmas tree?"

"Playing Santa again, Ryan?" She discarded the cup into a nearby trash bin. "How do you plan to get the tree to my house?"

He rapped the roof of his car. "I'll MacGyver it."

She eyed the roof rack. "I didn't know you skied."

He held the door for her as she slid inside. "Karen was big into going to the Wintergreen Ski Resort."

Karen... Anna clicked her seat belt in place, sorry she'd asked. He'd lived a whole life she knew nothing about.

And that bothered her. Which was unreasonable. Her baby only underscored the fact she'd lived a life totally unconnected to him, as well.

He steered past the nursery as the drive curved into the woodland. She studied him behind the wheel. Would he find happiness in his new job and fulfillment somewhere else? Had she found fulfillment?

Of course she had. Hadn't she? She faced out the window. Home at last, she had her baby. And her wonderful memories of Mateo. Yet suddenly, none of that felt enough. Not anymore.

Ryan parked between the farmhouse and barn. Judging from the number of cars, business was booming.

Anna waved to his youngest sister, Tessa, supervising the youngsters in the enclosed barnyard petting zoo. "It's busy today."

"For many families around here, it's become a tradition to bring the kids to Open House." He took stock of their hard work since his dad passed. "The farm is Luke's doing, a profitable year-round enterprise."

Sunbeams infused rich highlights in Anna's dark hair. "Year-round how?"

Anna was so lovely. He'd never imagined he'd ever be able to spend time with her again. But only until January, when their life paths diverged once more.

His chest tightened at the reminder. "In the spring, we grow flowers for the garden center. In the fall, we offer a corn maze and there's pumpkins for sale."

Tendrils of her hair skimmed her shoulders. "You don't fool me, Ryan." She wagged her finger. "Savages live, breathe and eat the farm."

He gestured toward the Christmas tree stand beside the red, Dutch hip-roofed barn. "In November, Luke travels to the Blue Ridge to get fresh-cut trees since the trees don't naturally grow in our salty climate."

At the sound of jingling bells, she turned to the old-fashioned sleigh. His other brother, Ethan, had a line of waiting customers.

Taking hold of her elbow, Ryan guided her over toward the sleigh. Children played hide-and-seek among the Christmas trees, positioned to resemble a real forest. An enchanted forest, especially with Anna by his side.

"Customers usually visit the petting zoo first, and then take a family sleigh ride before purchasing a tree."

With Tessa's old horse tied to the hitching post outside the barn, broad-shouldered Ethan helped his customers disembark from the sleigh. "Anna Banana! Good to have you home."

She made a wry grimace, but Ryan could tell she was pleased at Ethan's affectionate greeting. He and Ethan shared the tall Savage gene, but there the resemblance ended.

Ethan and Justine were blonder, their eyes bluer. And unlike Ryan, who tended to be more contemplative, Ethan was Mr. Never-Met-a-Stranger. Or had been until returning from his last deployment.

"It's good to be home." Anna ran her hand over the carriage frame. "This sleigh is new to me."

Ryan allowed the horse to nuzzle his hand. "Ethan's idea."

Ethan shook his head. "Ryan found the sleigh in the shed, tucked away for who knows how long. The leather had rotted. The runners broken. He restored the sleigh to its now pristine condition."

Ryan flushed. "We each did our part for the business."

"Don't be so modest, bro."

Her breath hitched softly. "Ryan, I had no idea you were so talented."

Ethan patted the horse's withers. "My brother is a handy guy to have around. Lots of hidden skills."

Ryan scowled. "Very hidden."

She ran her fingertip over the gold paint gilding the outline of the carriage. "This is beautiful." Her eyes shone. "Makes me want to break into a verse about dashing through the snow."

Ryan waggled his eyebrows. "Except in Kiptohanock, there isn't any snow."

Ethan handed an elderly lady into the carriage. "But brilliant as always, Ryan fixed wheels onto the runners to accommodate our sandy terrain."

Ryan surveyed the line of people. "Looks like you're booked solid."

Ethan unwound the reins from the post and placed them onto the driver's perch. "Come back later, and I'll give you the farm tour, Anna. Or better yet, Ryan can." He winked at his brother as he swung into the seat.

"I'd love that." Her gaze flickered to Ryan. "Maybe another day. Margaret mentioned something about costume fittings this afternoon, depending on when Tessa could get away."

Ethan took the reins. "I heard Ryan got shanghaied into the Living Nativity. Better him than me. Though I can't wait to see him in a dress."

"It's a robe, Ethan," Ryan growled. "Not a dress."

Ethan flicked the reins, and the sleigh rolled forward. "Whatever you say, big bro," he called over his shoulder. "Whatever you say."

She laughed. "The more things change, the more they remain the same."

He tugged her toward the tree stand. "Boring. Yet another reason to leave."

She shook her head. "Not boring. One of the things I love most about home."

And not so boring with Anna home. Doubts flooded Ryan. Had he somehow missed what God wanted for him?

Was he making a mistake in leaving the kids? And then there was Anna. Would he have pursued the job opportunity if he'd known she'd return to Kiptohanock?

Anna raised her hand. "Excuse me, Mister Sabbage?"

He grinned. "Yes, Anna Banana?"

Anna moistened her lips with her tongue. "May I be excused for a bathroom break?"

"Since you asked so nicely…" He motioned toward the restroom they'd installed for visitors. "Be my guest."

Anna fluttered her fingers as she headed toward the barn. "Thanks, friend."

Despite the blue sky and the brisk, autumn-tinged air, his spirits plummeted. They were just friends. He scrubbed his hand over his jaw. He was beginning to hate the phrase "just friends."

He needed to face reality. She didn't have room for anyone in her heart but the baby. And the past would always stand between them ever pursuing a relationship.

The breakup with Karen had left him leery of trusting his heart to another. Since then, only the kids had breached the barrier he'd erected around his heart. Already his feelings for Anna were more than he should feel for a friend, no matter how dear.

Feelings with the potential to exceed anything he ever felt for Karen. And that, ultimately, wasn't a path he'd willingly travel with Anna. Now more than ever, he needed to go off-Shore.

Because only an especially cruel heartache lay at the end of anything other than friendship with Anna. With everything awaiting him in his new job, to love Anna and her baby was a risk he couldn't afford.

Chapter Six

Minutes later, Anna ventured out of the barn at the Savage farm. She took a moment to enjoy the merriment of children scampering through the grove of Christmas trees. Families roamed, searching for the perfect tree. Older students greeted Ryan where he waited near the booth.

Strolling couples—perhaps their first Christmas together—underscored for Anna the coming loneliness of the life she'd chosen. She placed her hand atop her child to reassure herself as much as the baby.

As she approached, Ryan straightened. "Is this too much walking for you? Should we go back to the car?"

She started to tell him she'd changed her mind about finding a tree. But he appeared so happy showing her around his family farm, she didn't have the heart to cut short their adventure. "I'm fine. I want to get a tree today."

His brow creased. "Are you sure? Because we can do this another time."

But already the time seemed far too short. The time before the baby arrived. Time with Ryan. And once he left, she sensed their friendship would irrevocably change.

She needed to make the most of this carefree, spectacular day. Which was one of the hardest things she'd learned after Mateo died. That nothing lasted forever. She should enjoy her freedom from diapers, sleepless nights and worrying about the bills while she could.

Anna studied the man who cared enough to help her transition through the holiday. Handsome and caring. Ryan, her best friend forever.

Was that what forever looked like between her and Ryan? Friends only? That's what she wanted, right?

She swallowed. "Professionally speaking, which kind of tree do you recommend, Mister Sabbage?"

He gave her a slow smile. When her knees wobbled, his hand steadied her arm. Eliciting a wobbling of a different sort in her heart.

But then came a rippling movement within her womb. Her eyes widened, and her hand fell to her rounded abdomen.

"What's wrong?"

"Nothing's wrong." A prick of tears burned her eyelids. She smiled at him. "The baby moved."

He dropped his hand.

She blinked at his sudden reaction. He loved kids, yet he acted as if he were afraid of the baby. "What's the matter?"

His gaze fell to the ground. "Nothing. I just—"

"Anna!"

Florence Savage hurried out of the tree booth. Her frosted blond hair belied her sixty-something age.

Mrs. Savage enfolded her into an embrace. "You look stunning. Motherhood suits you, Anna Banana."

"You look marvelous, Mrs. Savage."

Behind his mother, Ryan made a face and rolled his eyes.

Without turning around, his mother fluttered her hand over her shoulder at Ryan. "Stop being a pest."

His mouth dropped open. "How did—?" He shook his head. "Never mind."

"Eyes in the back of my head, son. Essential skill for anyone in the teaching profession." She cupped Anna's cheek in her warm, dry palm. "Essential skill for motherhood, too."

Anna soaked in the tenderness in his mother's gaze. "Thank you for letting me know about the job."

Mrs. Savage patted Anna's cheek. "Your résumé and phone interview got the job."

Over the years, Ryan's mother had worked her way up the teaching ladder to become a high school principal. And she was a powerful champion for at-risk students in the community. Proving herself a great friend to Anna in her hour of need, too.

Seth Duer stepped out from the row of trees. "Aren't you supposed to be working the booth, Florence?"

Mrs. Savage arched her eyebrow. "Help Anna pick out a tree, Ryan, while I deal with this old coot."

"Who're you calling an old coot?" Seth Duer said, a smile playing around his mustached lips.

Anna wondered for a second... No way. Although, it had been a long time since Mr. Duer was widowed. She followed Ryan into the thicket of trees. "Your mom's been alone four years now?"

He paused to let a dad and his preschool daughter idle by. "Only if you don't count all five kids still living on the farm with her." His eyes cut to Anna's. "What a bunch of losers in the romance department, huh?"

She planted her hands on her hips. "The only people allowed to insult you, Ryan Savage, are me and your family. You're not a loser." She cocked her head. "Oblivious, maybe. A little slow..." She tapped her finger on her temple.

He lunged. "Says you—"

Squealing in feigned terror—as he meant her to—she darted behind a tree for cover. "You gotta catch me first, Savage," she yelled.

The old schoolyard game. Savages and Pruitts were frenemies from way back. Capture the flag without flags. A landlubber's version of catch and release.

"Ann...na..."

She smiled at his cajoling voice.

"Come out, come out wherever you are. Anna Ba... Nan...nah..."

His voice sounded farther away so she took off, zig-zagging between the rows. His boots thudded behind her.

Panting, she paused to regain her breath. Resting her hand on the spindly bark of a spruce, she blew a strand of hair out of her face. The bulb shape of the trees hid her ballooning belly.

"I'll find you." His voice drifted. "I always do..."

"Only 'cause I let you," she whispered.

The wind rustled the fragrant evergreen branches. And there were faint echoes from "other" children at play. She strained to hear his footsteps over the distant jingling on the sleigh harness.

An arm shot out from around the tree.

Squealing—this time not so feigned—she allowed her-self to be caught as he wrapped his hands around her upper arms. Her shoulder blades pressed against his chest, she closed her eyes, relishing the strength of his embrace. The wild thrumming of his heartbeat vibrated through her, matching the drumbeat of her own heart.

Grasping her shoulders, he gently angled her to face him. His eyes twinkled before another expression took its place. "Gotcha. As I knew I would." The blue-green of his eyes deepened.

"I knew you would, too." She forced the words from her constricted throat.

His hands framed her face. She nestled her cheek against the roughened texture of his palm. She'd always admired his hands. Manly, well formed. Not just the hands of a schoolteacher or researcher. Someone much more than she'd ever allowed herself to imagine.

Without conscious thought, she took a step closer. Her stomach rammed into him.

Flinching, he drew back. Taking a ragged breath, he tore his gaze away. "Sorry."

What was he sorry about? Sorry about almost starting something neither of them could finish? For one dizzying, terrifying second, she contemplated telling him—what?

What could she say? He finally had his chance to return to the work he loved. She should be relieved he had the good sense to stop whatever had been about to happen.

But why didn't she feel relieved?

His Adam's apple bobbed. "Let's find you a tree."

Of all the trees in the Enchanted Forest, she'd picked a scraggly, waist-high specimen.

"Seriously, Anna?" Ryan made a sweeping motion. "What about one of those bigger firs? Or one of the blue spruces? They're pretty."

Anna crossed her arms over her stomach and got that stubborn look in her eye. "I like this one."

He mirrored her stance. "It's not even shaped nice."

She stiffened. "I want this one."

He scrubbed his chin. Her likes and dislikes—as always—were a complete mystery to him.

She uncoiled. "I'll carry it out myself."

Ryan tugged her aside. "No one wants to have to deliver a baby today at Open House. I got this."

He hefted the potted tree. The branches slapped his cheek, and he spit out a mouthful of pine needles. He staggered toward the booth. She followed on his heels.

At the nearby baler, his youngest brother, Luke, hurried toward them. "Hey, Anna."

"Luke, tell Anna this is not the right tree for her. Tell her how this tree won't decorate pretty."

She jabbed her finger. "Luke, you tell *Ryan* it's *my* choice. And I choose this one. Tell him—"

"It's a Virginia pine." Luke's eyes flicked from Anna to Ryan. "The foliage will eventually become denser."

She folded her arms again. "I want this tree."

Ryan blew out a breath. "This isn't a cut tree, Anna. You're going to have to water this one."

"You have to put water in the base of cut trees, too." She tossed her hair over her shoulder. "I'll plant it. A tribute to my life before returning home."

His mouth thinned. "Where will you plant it? Outside that sorry excuse for a trailer you've rented?"

"Maybe I'll rent to own. What do you care? You won't be sticking around long enough to watch it grow." She glared at him. "Or anything else."

He raked his hand through his hair. "You're big on memorials, aren't you? Whatever happened to living in the present?"

Rising on her tiptoes, she got in his face. As much as the baby between them allowed. "You're a fine one to talk about the present when you can't wait to shake the sand off your feet."

Luke brushed his hand across the needles. "Don't judge this tree by its current appearance, bro. It's still in the process of becoming."

Her nostrils flared. "Totally."

Like Oscar, Maria and Zander. Like him?

His brother ran his finger along the reddish-brown trunk. "But it's also straight and true. No reason Anna can't plant it. By the fifth year of growth, this tree will be a gorgeous landscape addition."

She smirked. "You've just got to see its potential."

Was that his problem? Did he lack vision? Or was he fixed on the wrong vision of himself somewhere else? Without a caring adult in their lives, would the children ever fulfill their God-given potential? As for Anna...

Ryan folded his arms. "It's your Christmas. Your trailer."

"Yes, it is." She gave the netting machine the once-over. "Does it need wrapping?"

"The funnel shakes the tree of loose needles." Ryan glowered. "If Luke shakes this Charlie Brown wannabe, there won't be anything left to decorate."

Her brows lowered. "I love *this* tree."

Ryan scoured his neck with his hand. "I guess this is the one, then."

She fluttered her lashes. "Great." She wheeled around to Luke. "How shall we load it? Lash it to the top?"

Luke carried the tree to Ryan's car. "This should fit nicely in the lift back. What do you think, Ryan?"

Ryan opened the hatch.

"Or I'll bring my Beetle." She raised one eyebrow. "Wouldn't want to mar the pristine condition of Ryan's classic car."

Making it sound like he only cared about his car. When nothing could be further from the truth. He gritted his teeth and helped Luke secure the pot in the hatch.

She rummaged in her shoulder bag. "There wasn't a tag on the tree, Ryan. How much—?"

"This one's on the house." Ryan glowered.

Her lips flattened. "I can pay for my own Christmas tree."

For inexplicable reasons—he blamed it on pregnancy hormones—she acted like she wanted to pick a fight. And fighting was the last thing he wanted.

He jutted his jaw. "No charge."

Savages could out-stubborn a Pruitt any day of the week.

He clenched his teeth. "We couldn't give this tree away."

Glaring, she turned to his brother. "Luke?" A vein pulsed in her throat.

The shiest of the Savage siblings backed away, both hands raised. "Like Ryan says. You're doing us a favor."

She slung the purse strap over her shoulder. She marched toward the passenger side. "Since neither of you think my money is any good, it's time for me to head home. I'm more tired than I realized."

That made two of them.

He slammed the lift closed. The car rocked. "Whatever you say, Mrs. Reyes."

She scowled at him over the roof of the car.

Luke stuffed his hands in his pockets. "It was good to see you home again, Anna."

"Thank you, Luke." She glanced at Ryan. "I'm glad someone's happy I'm home." And she got into the car without another word.

Chapter Seven

Jaw clenched, Ryan carried the potted Christmas tree inside Anna's trailer. "Where do you want it?"

Lips tight, she pointed in front of the large window.

He wasn't feeling too positive about her right now, either. He hadn't remembered Anna being this stubborn. Good thing he was leaving in a few weeks. Only an idiot saw the hurt coming and kept running toward it.

As he drove away, he congratulated himself on dodging a bullet with Anna. Her situation wasn't his problem.

He had a job and a new life off-Shore. Life was simpler in the laboratory. Data collected. Data analyzed. Solution achieved. One plus one equaled two. Always. No deviation. Input yielded output every single time.

If only life was more like a formula. But relationships were messy. Fraught with complications and best avoided altogether. Anna was right. He wasn't going to stick around to watch a tree—or a baby—grow.

And what about the kids in the after-school program? The danger Oscar and his too-young mother faced every night in that sleazy motel nagged at Ryan.

Unable to quiet his heart, he called Agnes Parks with his concerns about Oscar. Twenty minutes later, he hung up with a sigh of relief. The problem had been identified. The problem would be resolved. His responsibility was done. For Anna, too.

And he kept telling himself that as a sleepless Saturday night rolled into Sunday morning. Right until he trudged into church and caught her watching for him.

His heart pounded. When his shadow fell over her, she glanced at him. And slid over a few inches on the wooden pew. Plenty of room for him. If that's what he wanted. He did.

Ryan sank into the pew. "Mornin', Anna." His voice sounded as raspy as fallen autumn leaves.

"Morning, Ryan."

Across the aisle with the rest of his siblings, Justine's mouth dropped open at his appearance. After an unsettled night, he was aware that not only did he look rough, he was also late for church. He raked his hand over his head, earning a concerned frown from his mother.

Pink, red and white poinsettias bedecked the altar steps. Each plant dedicated to the memory of an absent loved one. Including one for his father.

Christmas wasn't an easy time for his mom. Despite the shared merriment of the holiday—maybe *because* of it—Christmas could be an especially lonely time for those missing someone.

With sudden insight, he reckoned Anna must be experiencing a myriad of conflicting, confusing emotions. Joy at her child's impending birth coupled with the loss of the child's father.

The organ music swelled. Reverend Parks rose. Sweet sounds of Christmas filled the sanctuary. *O come all ye faithful*... The voices of the faithful floated toward the rafter beams. *Joyful and triumphant*...

He sighed. What was he doing with Anna? Why was he

getting involved with Oscar? There wasn't room in Anna's life for anyone except her child. He should be keeping his head down, his heart cordoned off and ticking down the days until the start of his new life. Anything else would not end well for him.

Come ye, oh come ye to Bethlehem... He stole a look at Anna. She sang, her hand resting atop her mushrooming abdomen. And then his eyes widened.

Like a fisted jab, the top of her stomach pulsed. From the inside, pushing outward. He blinked at the small, rounded bulge. The heel of a tiny foot or the imprint of a hand. In and out. In and out.

He counted the beats in his head. The movement in perfect rhythm with the organ music. Like a beater striking a kick drum.

O come let us adore Him... Was it possible? Did the unborn child hear the carol? His gaze returned to Anna's serene expression. Eyes closed, her head tipped back. Singing. Worshipping.

Perhaps Ryan had it wrong. Perhaps he'd always had it wrong. He wasn't done at all. Not with Oscar. Not with Maria and Zander.

Ryan's stomach knotted. *O come let us adore Him...* His attention, yet again, was drawn to the pulsing rhythm of the baby in Anna's womb. Perhaps the real truth was Ryan had no room in his heart for anyone but himself.

Help me, God. I don't know what You want me to do.

But maybe deep down, Ryan already knew what God wanted him to do. Did loving God mean loving His children also? He sucked in a breath. Was that what God wanted of him? To love Maria, Oscar and Zander? Anna's baby, too?

Something shifted inside him. And though he had no idea how—somehow he trusted all would be well. The next month might not unfold the way he first envisioned, but walking away was not going to be an option for him. He had to be in this for Anna and the kids for the duration. At least, until Christmas.

The congregation finished with a triumphant flourish as the last chords of the organ died away.

Anna leaned close. "Are you okay?" she whispered.

He nodded before sinking into the seat. He had a hard time focusing on the sermon. And after the final benediction, she touched his sleeve. "I'm sorry for what happened yesterday."

Whereas he'd been sorry about what hadn't happened.

His shoulders hunched. Was that true? Since renewing their friendship, he'd rationalized he could remain friends with Anna and require nothing more. But after yesterday at the tree farm?

Ryan wasn't so sure he could be this close to her and be content with friendship. Anna and the kids were like a battering ram against the walls of his heart. And with every encounter, his defensive barricades weakened a little more.

He might not be able to completely walk away, but he could spend less time with her. Establish better boundaries with Anna. For the welfare of his heart.

"Ryan, I want you to know how grateful I am for everything you've done for me."

"Grateful…" Like forcing down a bitter pill, he swallowed hard. "Right."

This was a Ryan problem. Not an Anna problem.

She worried her lower lip with her teeth. "I hate to be a pest, but…could you fix the lock for me this week?"

The thought crossed his mind that she was searching for a reason to see him again. As if she was afraid she'd pushed him too far. Asked for one favor too many. But he had promised to fix the lock on the trailer door.

"Tomorrow after school?" Her voice grew small. "Ryan?"

He never could say no to her. "Okay."

So much for boundaries.

But at least this way, he could keep an eye on her without offending her pride or antagonizing her independent spirit. For the baby's sake. He grimaced. A poor excuse was better than none.

"Thank you, Ryan." The dazzling brilliance of her smile momentarily blinded him.

He walked her outside, careful not to touch her. That's where he'd gone wrong yesterday. New rule—no unnecessary touching.

At the edge of the winter-brown grass, she moved toward her car. She waved as she slipped into the Volkswagen. And he watched her drive away.

Maybe that's what this was about. A lesson in letting her go. He could do that. Couldn't he? He'd let her go once before when they went their separate ways after high school. He clenched his eyes shut.

But the real question? If this time he could let her go without falling helplessly and hopelessly in love with her.

Chapter Eight

At lunch on Monday, Anna rubbed her aching back before settling into the chair at the teacher table. For the first time that day, she caught a glimpse of Ryan. He strolled the perimeter of the cafeteria on lunch duty.

Once in a while, he leaned over to speak to a particular student. He patted others on the shoulder. Good-naturedly ruffling the hair on some of the boys. Who grinned and pointed stubby fingers at Ryan's perpetually rumpled hair.

He was so good with them. She found it hard to imagine Ryan as a man meant to spend his days in the sterile, white-coat environment of a lab. Over jeans, he wore an open-collared dress shirt underneath a brown suede blazer with elbow patches. Just the right mixture of professionalism and approachability.

Sipping from her water bottle, she was chagrined when he didn't stop to say hello. Or smile at how she'd braided her hair this morning. Why had she bothered? And why did it bother her so much he hadn't noticed?

Anna got up and stood at the table of squirming five-year-olds. She raised her hand to get their attention. The students fell silent, their eyes on her. She reminded them to properly dispose of their trash before lining up to return to the classroom.

When the children scattered to do as she asked, she headed toward the exit doors to wait. But even before she heard his voice—by the tingling between her shoulder blades—she felt Ryan standing behind her.

"Anna Banana…" he whispered.

Pivoting, she gave in to the urge to smile.

"Are we still on for this evening?" His voice was ultra-casual, but his eyes were not.

Her insides turned to mush. "With bells on." Since church yesterday, she'd thought of nothing but him.

Ryan's lips quirked. "Sleigh bells?"

"You still owe me a sleigh ride." She toyed with a tendril of hair around her earlobe. "And one day, I aim to collect."

His gaze followed the movement of her hand. "You did something different to your hair."

She bit her lip. "Do you like it?"

His eyes traveled from her hair to her mouth. "Your hair is beautiful however you choose to wear it, Anna." Their gazes locked for an instant until one of his students called for him and he turned away.

That afternoon, she began a unit on holiday traditions around the world. Isaac Finkelstein's mother was coming tomorrow to talk about Hanukkah. Other parents would do likewise over the coming weeks. On the last day before winter break, she planned to surprise her students with a star piñata at the holiday party.

She incorporated the same lesson plans in her literacy work with Oscar, Maria and Zander after school. She started with the Mexican traditions Mateo's grandmother had taught him. About the *posadas*—processions venturing to different homes each night in the nine days leading to Christmas. Together they read the folktale about the *flor de nochebuena*—the Christmas poinsettia.

After the children finished their work with Agnes and Ryan, she asked Maria to share about her family's holiday traditions. Nervous and soft-spoken at first, her voice became animated as she told them about the *nacimiento*—how a different member in the nativity tableau was added each day until on Christmas Eve the Christ Child was placed in the manger. Even Zander listened without interrupting or making wisecracks, a hint of wistfulness on his face.

Later at the trailer, she combed her fingers through the woven strands of her braid. She changed into a more comfortable top and, in a task getting trickier by the day, put on a pair of holiday-green elf socks.

She heard a tread on the porch steps outside. "Come in," she called. Her hair fell in crinkly waves across her shoulders.

Gripping a toolbox, Ryan pushed open the door. "You really shouldn't leave the door unloc—" He froze, his eyes fixed on the sway of her tresses.

"Ryan?"

He jolted at the sound of her voice. "I—I got caught by a parent. Sorry I'm later than expected." Turning away, he gave her a nice view of his back as he jiggled the doorknob.

But not before she'd seen the spark in his eyes. Ryan Savage liked her hair to hang long. Her pulse skittered, and she filed the information away for future reference. Gratified in a way she didn't completely understand. Or cared to probe too deeply.

She willed her heartbeat to settle. "Charlie installed motion sensor lights on the trailer."

Ryan sank to his knees in front of the door and opened

his toolkit. "Sounds like Charlie has taken care of everything you need."

She pursed her lips at his flannel-clad back. Unsure from his tone if he sounded relieved or distressed.

Refusing her offer of assistance, he also installed a dead bolt. "Agnes and I plan to visit Oscar's mom during my planning period tomorrow to see if she can shed any light on Oscar's fatigue."

Anna smiled. "I knew you'd know how to best handle the situation."

He shook his head. "Agnes has the social work background, not me. And as the pastor's wife, she has connections. She's the perfect one to get involved with this. Especially since I'm leaving soon."

Anna frowned.

He installed the last screw. "Voilà!" He stepped out onto the stoop and shut the door with a click.

She laughed when he knocked. In her stocking feet, she plodded to the door. "Who is it?"

"It's me." A muffled reply.

She grinned. "Me who?"

"The me who's freezing out here in the cold."

She swung wide the door. His glasses fogged from the warmth inside the trailer. As his glasses slowly cleared, he gave an elaborate shiver. She rolled her eyes.

He handed her the new key. "All done." He shrugged into his brown Carhartt jacket. "I better call it a night."

Blinking rapidly, she assessed the shabby trailer, seeking inspiration. "Wait."

He zipped his jacket. "Was there something else you needed, Anna?"

She needed his company, his good humor and his friendship more than anything else in the world. But she couldn't say that to him. Her pride battled against her need for Ryan to want to spend time with her. And not because he believed she was a charity case.

"What about the back door?" She raised her palms to shoulder level. "Don't you think you ought to inspect that lock, too? To be on the safe side?"

His brow creased. "Okay…"

Leading him toward the hallway off the living room, she flipped on a light.

Bending, he examined the lock. "You're right. It does need replace—"

"When?"

"—cing." The bridge between his eyes furrowed into a V.

She tamped down her enthusiasm. She was almost a mother. She had to maintain a certain dignity. "How about tomorrow?"

He rubbed his scruffy jaw with his hand. For a moment, she was certain he was going to refuse. Her gut twisted. Her heart sank. She held her breath.

"Sure." He raked his hand over his head. "I've got a committee meeting, but afterward…"

Anna gave him the full-fledged version of the renowned Pruitt smile. A charm Charlie had used with potent effect to win the heart of Kiptohanock librarian, Evy.

Ryan rocked slightly on the heels of his brogans. Then he headed for the front door. Giddy with relief, she padded along behind him.

Hand on the newly installed doorknob, he gave her a stern, fifth-grade teacher look. "Set the bolt after I leave, Anna."

She gave him a two-fingered salute. "Will do, Mister Sabbage, sir."

His eyebrows rose. "Are you feeling all right, Anna?"

"Never better." Totally, surprisingly true. She couldn't remember the last time she felt this good.

With one foot in and one foot out the door, Ryan hesitated. "See you tomorrow."

She hung on to the door. "Can't wait."

And that truth kept her awake long past her bedtime.

On Tuesday morning, the motel looked no better than it had Friday night. Maybe even worse. Daylight only emphasized the peeling paint, the pitted parking lot and the sagging eaves.

With a click on his key fob, Ryan locked his car. "Not the safest place, Mrs. Parks."

Agnes walked with him toward the entrance. "I've seen worse."

He inclined his head. "When you worked for social services?"

She gave him a small smile. "No. As a pastor's wife. My husband's work isn't just on Sunday. We both take our commitment to the community very seriously."

He'd done the right thing in bringing Mrs. Parks here. She and the Reverend had the background, the knowledge and the wherewithal to do what needed to be done for Oscar.

"And this is the only address you found listed in his school record? I thought Oscar's mom worked the night shift?"

He held the glass-fronted door for Agnes. "It's the only address I found. No other phone number listed. I hope we can get a permanent address and contact number from the manager."

But when they ventured inside, once again Brittany Ericson stood behind the counter. He searched her face for telltale signs of drug abuse. If she was using, he'd call Child Protective Services immediately.

"You again." Her eyes cut to Agnes. "Who are you?"

Oscar's mother had the skeletal thinness of an addict, but her teeth weren't yellowed and she didn't have the shakes.

She frowned at his scrutiny, then her eyes widened. "Did something happen to Oscar?"

"Oscar is fine." Agnes smiled. "He's with his class at school."

"So, why are you here? I ain't got all day to shoot the breeze with you people." Brittany glanced around as if expecting someone to interrupt. "I'm on the clock."

His fears for Oscar rose another notch. "Do you work here all the time?" He wasn't sure how to phrase this without offending her. Though offending her was the least of Oscar's worries. "By the hour?"

Brittany's eyes glinted. "Yes. No. Not in the way you mean."

Agnes held out her hand. "I'm Agnes Parks, and I also work in the after-school program with your son."

Brittany locked her arms around herself. "What do you want?" Agnes's hand fell.

Ryan cleared his throat. "We're concerned about how tired Oscar is at school every day." He surveyed the dingy lobby. "Is this where Oscar sleeps every night?"

Brittany glared. "I know it ain't much, but it's a job. I'm doing the best I can."

Agnes stepped closer. "I'm sure you are, Brittany. We're trying to do what's best for Oscar, too."

Brittany's thin shoulders slumped. "That's why you're here, isn't it?" Her voice dropped. "You're here to take Oscar away from me."

Ryan started to speak, but Agnes's hand on his arm

stopped him. "Is that what you think would be best for your son, Brittany?"

"F-first week I got the job—" Brittany's voice quavered "—a rat crawled across Oscar."

Ryan's stomach clenched.

"He wasn't bitten, I checked. But he's terrified of them now. So I keep him near me behind the desk. There's all kinds of rats out there." She glanced toward the parking lot. "Not only the rodent kind. I can't risk putting him in one of the empty rooms to sleep by himself."

Ryan sucked in a breath. Other than her job at the motel, Oscar and his mom were homeless.

Brittany lifted her chin, her jaw like iron. "I sleep during the day. So I can stay awake and make sure nothing gets on Oscar. But he won't let himself go to sleep." She choked, a half sob. "He sleeps at school where he feels safer."

Ryan's heart clenched for the scared little boy. "Let us help, Brittany."

The defiance seemed to drain out of her. "Don't you think I've considered giving him up?" She looked at them, all traces of hardness gone. "But would foster care be better? You tell me." She snorted. "How do you think I ended up pregnant at fifteen with Oscar in the first place?"

Something tore inside Ryan for a young woman who'd already suffered so much. "Let us help you, too, Brittany."

"There's no help for someone like me." She shrugged as if she didn't care, but tears welled in her eyes. "I'm broken beyond fixing."

Agnes took Brittany's fist in her hand. "Nobody's broken beyond fixing. I know a lady looking for a boarder. We can find you a new place to live. A safer place."

Brittany shook her head. "I can't afford—"

"How would you like to work in a garden center?"

As soon as the words left his mouth, he was appalled at himself.

But Agnes gave him a pleased smile. Luke was going to have his head on a Christmas platter.

The family had just started to dig themselves out from a financial hole. Ryan gritted his teeth. But somehow, somewhere, they'd find a way to pay Brittany more than the paltry amount she had to be making here.

Brittany's mouth curved. "I like plants." Then her eyes dulled. "But I don't have a car."

Agnes shooed away her concerns. "Transportation can be arranged. Trust me."

Trust was the crucial issue. Would Brittany trust them? But trust went both ways. Ryan had to be willing to trust this young woman with something more important to him than the business: his family.

Brittany tilted her head. "Are you sure?"

His family wouldn't want Ryan to deny them the chance to make a difference in Brittany's life. Justine and Tessa would have a ball loving on little Oscar. Their mom, too.

Ryan nodded. "I'm sure."

Agnes moved into action. "Let's get you packed."

"Thank you." A smile flickered across Brittany's face. "For everything. I never dreamed——" She blinked back tears.

His heart lifted at the hope dawning on the young woman's features. It didn't take long for Brittany to pack. The entirety of her and Oscar's possessions were contained in a single backpack.

Ryan drove them to the school parking lot to retrieve Agnes's car. With his planning period nearly over, Agnes would take it from here. By the end of the day, Brittany would be settled into a new place. And tonight, he hoped Oscar would have sweet dreams at last.

Hurrying into the school building, Ryan had a phone call to make to his brother. But he felt better than he had in a long time. As if one of the weights lodged on his shoulders had lifted. He could leave with a clear conscience. He'd done what he could for Oscar and his mom. Done everything he could for everyone.

Or had he? Zander and Anna rose to his mind. And suddenly he had the uncomfortable suspicion that leaving here wasn't going to be as easy as he once believed.

That afternoon, while Ryan worked to secure the lock on the back door of the trailer, Anna—oh so casually—mentioned the lack of a peephole.

She gave him the bright Pruitt smile. "Then I wouldn't have had to guess it was you knocking on the door last night."

Obviously, she'd known it was Ryan on the other side of the door.

He stared at her over the rim of his glasses. And she feared he'd call her on the absurdity of her request. But he cocked his head in that way he had of studying a question from every angle.

"Okay…" He blew out a breath. "I'll fix that next."

She leaned forward, resisting the urge to do a fist-pump. "Wednesday?"

When he agreed without further questions, she released the breath she hadn't realized she'd been holding.

On Wednesday, the mellow sound of "Have Yourself a Merry Little Christmas" filled the small trailer while Ryan worked on the peephole.

In the frayed upholstery of an armchair, her candy cane–striped stocking feet dangled over the armrest. She sipped from a mug of herbal tea. And—thanks to Ryan—this Christmas was shaping up to be a merry one.

On Thursday, she roped him into hanging swags of garland. A garland that new employee Brittany Ericson rang up for Anna at the garden center.

The transformation in Oscar was remarkable. Within a few days, he went from a withdrawn, sleep-deprived child to a bubbly, curious six-year-old, eager to learn. Which was exactly what he should be.

Although Ryan insisted he'd done very little, Anna almost burst with how proud she was of Ryan for his part in giving Oscar and his mom a new start.

A new start. What Anna had hoped for when she returned home to raise her child.

That her new beginning and Oscar's took place during the holiday season was icing on the cake. A Christmas cake. And how much of her happy Christmas homecoming she owed to Ryan both scared and thrilled Anna.

With the upcoming Kiptohanock tree lighting ceremony on Friday night, she and Ryan decided to make good on their promise of a reward for the effort put forth by the kids. Permission from Maria's family and Oscar's mom was easily acquired. But Anna had no success in contacting Zander's guardian.

Just when she worried he'd have to be left behind, Zander arrived at the media center on Friday afternoon and dug the crumpled form from his backpack. Broadening his stance, he handed it to her.

Chin raised, he folded his arms. A fair imitation of the way Ryan often stood. Ryan had no clue what a positive masculine influence he presented to boys like Zander.

"You said we'd eat at Tammy and Johnny's first, right? And my milkshake is free, too."

She scanned the permission slip. "I can't read your guardian's name on the signature line."

His lips flattened. "I did what you said. Got it signed. Can I go or what?"

Although grubby and smudged, it appeared the official requirements had been met. If only they could as easily find a solution for his behavioral issues.

She turned the paper over in her hand. "Your address isn't listed."

He shrugged, the chip on his shoulder growing exponentially. "My uncle said he'd drop me at the restaurant."

An uncle. Maybe now they might get somewhere. Finally, a chance to talk to an adult in Zander's life. "I look forward to meeting him. What's your uncle's name?"

He picked up a book lying on the table. "What chapter did you say we were working on today?"

She wasn't fooled. Zander looked forward to reading every day as much as someone awaiting a tray full of vaccinations. Something was up with him. Her suspicions aroused, she meant to get to the bottom of it tonight.

Chapter Nine

Ryan took Friday off from school. A self-imposed distance. Thus far, his decision to avoid her wasn't working. He'd spent way more time with Anna than was good for his heart. And the close proximity wasn't doing anything for his so-called boundaries. He needed to draw a line in the proverbial Kiptohanock sand.

Which—considering he was about to spend Friday evening with Anna and the kids at the tree lighting—was a half-hearted, doomed-to-failure attempt at best.

But nonetheless late that afternoon, he found himself winding a strand of white lights around the town gazebo railing. Something his dad had volunteered for each year. A job that, oddly enough, made him feel closer to his dad. But this was the last year he'd be home to decorate the square.

Margaret Davenport supervised the volunteers like a general marshaling her troops. Four different groups trimmed a tree on each corner of the green. Tonight marked the Kiptohanock Tree Lighting. And Margaret was here to make sure everything was done to her usual high standards for the little fishing village. She marched across the square to harangue the Waterman's Association—mainly Seth Duer—in charge of the tree closest to the church.

Ryan worked the lights around the railing spindles, and his defense mechanisms went around, as well. They were just friends. *Can't get attached.* He was leaving soon. They were just friends. *Can't get attached.* He was leaving—

At the clatter on the roof of the gazebo, he poked his head out. Glad for a distraction, he grinned at the teenager climbing the aluminum ladder. "Santa? So soon? I'm not ready."

"You better get ready, Mr. Savage." An electrical cord dangled from the Moravian Christmas star in Gray Montgomery's hand. "'Cause Santa Claus is coming to town." He smirked. "Even a town the size of Kiptohanock."

"Better heed your own advice, son." Canyon Collier braced the bottom of the ladder against the gazebo. "Santa knows when you've been bad or good. So—"

Ryan wagged his finger. "—be good for goodness sake." Exchanging glances, he and Canyon burst out laughing.

Gray heaved a sigh. "Old people humor." He stretched to attach the star onto the top of the gazebo.

Canyon sucked in a breath as Gray wobbled. "Careful..."

Ryan's eyes darted from Gray's precarious perch to Canyon's face.

"I got this, dude," Gray called. "No worries."

"Fear is so not a factor." Canyon shook his head. "Do you remember being immortal when you were sixteen, Ryan?"

Gray teetered.

"Stop fooling around, son." Canyon's face reflected his concern.

Ryan jammed his hands into the warmth of his coat pockets. "Gray won the prize this year to install the star?"

"More like the short straw." Canyon gestured. "My son

was thrilled for the opportunity to defy the laws of gravity."

Gray wasn't Canyon's son, though. He was his stepson, Kristina's son by her first marriage to an airman killed over Afghanistan.

Ryan fingered the stubble on his chin. "That's kind of rich coming from a crop duster like you."

Canyon's mouth curved. "Aerial application specialist."

Ryan chuckled. "Sorry. I forgot. My bad."

Canyon exhaled. "You can't fault the boy. Take your pick. Nature or nurture."

Ryan arched his eyebrow. "Either way, he didn't stand a chance of avoiding the daredevil gene."

Canyon glanced over his shoulder toward the florist shop. "Just don't tell his mother. She'd have a fit." He sniffed. "You know how women worry."

Ryan had difficulty not cracking a smile. "I hear you, man. *They* do worry about every little thing."

Canyon laughed. "That they do."

"I've been wondering…" Ryan shuffled his feet. "Feel free to tell me to mind my own business."

"Fire away. I won't answer if I don't like the question."

Ryan took a breath. "You and Gray are close. You and your niece, too. Neither of them are your biological children. And now that Kristina is carrying your child—"

"Won't make any difference." Canyon never took his eyes off Gray. "It doesn't work like that. Or at least not for me."

"How does it work then?"

"Does this have anything to do with Anna Reyes?"

Ryan didn't answer, but red crept from beneath his collar.

"Thought so." Canyon's mouth twitched. "Therefore, I

expect you're not asking out of nosiness but out of a need to know."

"Anna and I are old friends," Ryan mumbled, his lips suddenly stiff from the cold.

Canyon cut his eyes at Ryan. "Sure you are. Friends make the best—"

"Woo-hoo!" Gray fist-pumped the sky. "Mission accomplished."

Canyon motioned. "Good for you. Now climb down slowly off the roof." He stepped aside as Gray moved down the rungs. "Get your buddies to help you return the ladder to the fire station."

Jumping the last two feet, Gray landed as nimbly as only a sixteen-year-old could and wheeled toward a group of kids Ryan recognized from the youth group.

Canyon smiled. "I couldn't love Gray or Jade more if they were my biological children."

"But he'll never be your son." Ryan's heart thundered. "Don't you see his father every time you look at him?"

"Love doesn't work like that." Canyon's blue eyes sharpened. "Paxton Montgomery's love for Kristina and Gray made them who they are today. As for the unpredictable, always marvelous purple-haired girl of mine?" His face brightened. "Every day I think how blessed I am to have them in my life."

"But how do you get there? I want to, but..." Ryan dropped his gaze.

"It's like Paxton passed me the torch. And God's given me the sacred privilege to finish ráising his son. A gift of grace—nothing I ever deserved. Same with Jade."

"What about your own child when he or she is born?"

Canyon's shoulders rose and fell. "They're all my children, Ryan. This child Kristina carries..." He swallowed. "An unexpected gift I never thought would be mine."

Ryan sighed. "It still doesn't add up to me."

"Sometimes love makes no sense. Love multiplies as it's given. Never divides. I can't explain it. I just know it's so."

"Dad!" Hands cupped around her mouth, Jade stood on the sidewalk in front of the florist shop. "Dad! Mom needs you!"

Canyon waved. "Gotta go. I'd be happy to talk more another time." He winked at Ryan. "But right now, love is calling."

Ryan finished installing the lights. He planned to drive Anna to the tree lighting later. Her vehicle was high on his To-Fix list, except she kept throwing other projects his way. As for the children? Agnes was bringing Oscar and his mom.

Thanks to an introduction by the Reverend, Maria's father had a new job as Mr. Keller's ranch foreman. Mr. Guzman would take care of the horses during the off-season and help run the foster kids camp in the summer. Maria's mom would take care of Mr. Keller. With Mr. Keller getting on in years, the family moved into the big house with him. The Guzmans were driving into town with the old man.

Anna had texted him about Zander meeting them at the restaurant. Ryan sighed. The kid worried him.

There was something he couldn't quite put his finger on with Zander. Anna had agreed. Something they were both missing. But hopefully in meeting Zander's uncle tonight, they could gain more clarity into his situation.

Ryan crossed the square to his car. As for what the evening possibly held for him and Anna?

It was getting harder and harder to deny the attraction he felt for her. He grimaced. They were just friends. *Can't get attached.* He was leaving soon.

Leaving too soon? He scrubbed his hand over his face. Or not soon enough?

Zander and his uncle never showed.

Anna and Ryan waited an hour at the restaurant, sending the Guzmans and the Ericsons ahead to save them a spot at the tree lighting ceremony.

Finally on the village green, Ryan's breath frosted in the wintry air. "If I had any idea where he lived, I'd—" His jaw clenched.

"Me, too." She huddled into the warmth of her coat. "Maybe something came up. A reason his uncle couldn't bring him. Or maybe Zander changed his mind about coming."

Ryan blew on his cold fingers. "Is that what you really think?"

She shook her head. "No." Zander had been especially self-controlled and diligent over the past week. He'd been desperately sincere—and for once very childlike—in his desire to attend the tree lighting.

Ryan's eyes clouded. "If nothing else, Zander's not the type to lose the chance for a free milkshake."

"What should we do?"

Her heart hurt from fretting about the whereabouts of the third grader. Was he sobbing somewhere because one more adult had let him down? Hungry because no one cared enough to make sure he got something to eat?

"There's nothing we can do about it now." Ryan hunched his shoulders. "Try not to worry."

She stepped closer. "Like you're not worrying?"

"We'll sort it out with him on Monday. Give him another reward." Ryan's lips tightened. "A reward within our control."

Using Ryan as a windbreak, she nestled against his

side. "Brrrr." It was nice leaning into him. Relying on his wisdom and strength instead of having to shoulder everything alone.

"Are you cold?" His arm went around her shoulders. Almost immediately, though, he dropped it. "Sorry." He inserted a breath of space between them.

She regretted more than the loss of his warmth. But she couldn't say that, of course. They were friends. She shouldn't expect anything more. She was being foolish. Tears burned her eyelids.

Hormones. She sniffed. She needed to get her act together. Ryan was leaving soon. She had to face facts. But it was a reality that caused her chest to ache.

"When, Mama?" Oscar, the human pogo stick, plucked at his mother's coat sleeve. "When?"

Brittany smiled at her son. "Soon," she whispered. "Good things come to those who wait. Right, Mrs. Reyes?"

Anna nodded, and the pressure eased at Brittany's soft-spoken reminder. They waited with most of the year-round residents for the lights of a Kiptohanock Christmas to shine forth on the darkened square.

High overhead, stars glittered in the velvety blackness of the December evening. Ryan hummed a Christmas song. She shouldn't get too used to Ryan. Who lately seemed so much more than a friend.

She nudged him. "You sound happy."

"It's the most wonderful time of the year. How about you?"

She blushed. "Yes," she whispered. "I am." More than she would've believed possible a few weeks ago.

He gave her that lopsided smile of his. And something fluttered in her chest.

"Good." His eyes crinkled. "My job is done."

She bristled. Was that what she was to him? A job.

For more than the usual reasons, this year she'd come to dread contemplating the day after Christmas. Ryan would be gone. And whatever she'd be doing, she'd be doing alone.

"About that…"

He glanced at her.

"After the tree lighting, would you come back to the trailer?"

He pursed his lips. "I do have to drive you home."

"I meant to watch a Christmas movie with me."

He frowned. A long moment in which she had difficulty drawing in a breath of air. Finally—

"Okay." He tugged the end of her red tartan scarf. "Unless it's one of those sappy chick flicks."

Blissful relief.

"Oh." She grabbed his coat. "Look."

Sudden light blazed from the four corners of the square. Atop the gazebo, the star burned brightly, pushing away the inky blackness of the night. Gasps of delight echoed around the green. Maria clapped her little brother's hands together. And Oscar's eyes weren't the only ones shining.

Thanks to a heads-up by Agnes and Reverend Parks, the Ericsons and the Guzmans soon found themselves knee-deep in a crowd of town residents eager to make their acquaintance. She and Ryan called out their goodbyes as they ambled toward his car.

Gratitude flooded her heart. It was so good to be home, a place where people cared about each other. Good ole Kiptohanock.

She stole a look at Ryan as they drove out of the village over the small bridge. Was it gratitude she felt for him?

At the trailer, she set a bag of popcorn inside the microwave. Over the last week, she'd glimpsed snatches of the loneliness Ryan did his best to hide from family and friends.

But she saw through his busyness to his heart. She'd always been able to see through the shields he erected. To the real Ryan. He was going to make some woman—

She clenched her eyes shut against an image of Ryan loving someone else. Of being loved by someone else. When he left soon… Her throat caught. Not seeing him would be excruciating.

Every day she promised herself she'd back away from Ryan. Yet every night she couldn't go through with her plan to wean herself from spending time together. Instead, she baited him with yet another project.

Making it harder for him to eventually leave. To leave the kids. To leave her. But each evening when he finished her latest To-Do item, her resolve weakened. Her palms became clammy. She actually felt dizzy. And she found herself cajoling him back again.

The microwave dinged. She shook herself. She had to stop needing him. Tonight, she had to let him go. Set him free to live the life he most wanted. She was being selfish.

If she truly loved him… She yanked open the microwave. Loved? Grabbing the popcorn bag, she slammed the microwave door shut.

Of course she loved him. She'd loved Ryan Savage since they were six years old. He was her best friend.

"Everything okay in there, Anna Banana?" he called from the living room.

She gritted her teeth as she tore into the bag and dumped the contents into a large plastic bowl. "Almost ready."

Which was another lie. She wasn't ready to say goodbye to Ryan. Clutching the bowl against her chest, she headed to the living room, where he crouched before the television.

Glancing up, he smiled. She ignored the flurry in her

pulse that his smile ignited. She opened her mouth to speak, but Ryan beat her to the punch.

"How about we do a Walmart run tomorrow?"

She pressed her lips together.

Hands on his knees, he shifted his weight. "Get some stuff for the baby just in case."

She blinked. "Just in case what?"

Rising, he took the bowl from her. "While you have me here to help you. So you don't have to deal with it alone after I move."

"I—"

He held up his hand. "Before you go ballistic on me, Mom and the sisters are bugging me to find out what you need for the baby. Since you wouldn't let the church ladies give you a baby shower." He gave her a look. "You'd be doing me a favor by getting them off my back."

"Okay."

"'Cause if it's one thing I don't need is a bunch of hens—wait." He cocked his head. "Did you say yes?"

With only the bowl—and the baby—between them, she had a hard time remembering to breathe. "I'd love to go shopping with you." She headed to the seen-better-days sofa. "I'm female, aren't I?"

He flopped on the couch beside her. "Never been a question about that."

She took the bowl before he spilled the popcorn.

He snagged a handful of kernels. "What's on tonight?"

She scrounged under the cushion for the remote and handed it to him. "My favorite. *It's a Wonderful Life.*"

"My favorite, too."

She swallowed. "I remember."

He munched on popcorn while they watched the movie. Kicking off his shoes, his long legs stretched out on the braided rug. During the commercials, he crooned familiar holiday jingles to car dealerships and department store ads.

"You are insane." But she laughed as he meant her to. Egging him on further. Such a guy. She grinned.

Tiring of holding the popcorn, she rested the half-empty bowl on top of her belly. Her stomach rippled. And a tiny, rounded punch sent the bowl sailing off the couch.

She gasped as the popcorn went flying. The bowl landed on the rug with a thud. "Did you see that?"

He bent over her abdomen. "Way to go, little bit. Tell your mama you're not a table." He touched his hand to her belly.

Another thump. He sucked in a breath and removed his hand.

"The baby knows your voice, Ryan."

His forehead wrinkled. "You think?"

"I do." She seized his hand and pressed his palm against her side. "Do it again. Say something."

For a second, he resisted the pressure of her hand. But leaning closer, he sang a line from "The Little Drummer Boy." "Pa-rumm-pa-rumm-pumm."

A one-two punch crested like a wave across her abdomen.

He bit his lip. "It's because I'm a guy. Like you'd hear a bass thrumming in a monitor."

She shook her head. "The baby's never done that with anyone else but me. And my voice isn't as deep as yours."

"You really think the baby likes me?"

She tilted her chin. "What's not to like?"

His gaze lifted to hers. Her heart pounded at his expression. Fire and ice. Like a sweep of snowflakes dancing across her skin. Like the flame of a candle burning in an otherwise dark night.

When another wave of motion crested across her belly, the moment was lost.

Moving his hand to the new location, Ryan's face transformed. "Hello, little one." A somersault this time.

She laughed, but tears swam in her eyes. "Baby says hello to you, too."

"You're going to have a wonderful life, little one." His eyes gleamed behind his glasses. "Such a wonderful life, Anna."

And for the first time since she buried Mateo, she believed it just might be true.

Chapter Ten

At Walmart the next day, Ryan held up two diaper bags. "Take your pick, Anna Banana."

Resting against the handle of the shopping cart, she touched her finger to her chin. "I like the black polka-dot one. *Très chic.*"

He tossed it into the growing pile of purchases. Stunned at the amount of stuff babies required.

She frowned. "Are you keeping a tally against how much your mom gave you?"

He reached for a Diaper Genie on a nearby shelf. "Don't worry about it." He loaded the large box into the cart.

"That's too expensive. Ryan…" She tapped her foot on the store linoleum. "Are you listening to me?"

Somebody ought to tell her how cute she looked aggravated and pregnant. Somebody. Not him. He was leaving in a few weeks. And he preferred not to dwell on that moment last night when she'd looked at him.

Ryan lifted something labeled a onesie. "How about this?"

She gave him one of her best teacher looks.

"You realize since I'm a teacher myself, those looks bounce right off me."

She arched her eyebrow and grinned.

In a mild state of shock, he realized it was the first time he'd self-identified as a teacher. Not a research scientist.

To be on the safe side—and to give himself time to recover—he tossed in two onesies.

"You're going to buy everything, aren't you?" She blew out a long, slow trickle of air between those beautiful, plum-tinted lips of hers. "No matter if I protest or not."

He grabbed a package of pacifiers. "I'm enjoying myself."

She tilted her head. "Of course, there's one thing I haven't figured out about you."

He smirked. "I'm amazed there's only one thing."

Anna leaned her elbows on the cart. "I haven't figured out why you've never asked."

Slam-dunking the pacifiers into the cart, he reached for a set of bibs. "Asked what?"

"The baby's gender."

His pulse zipped. "Didn't figure it mattered. Didn't realize you knew." He studied the directions on a baby monitor as if his life depended on it.

"Do you want to know?"

Ryan's heart hammered. Yes, he wanted to know the identity of the little person to whom he was becoming too attached.

He took a ragged breath. No, he didn't want to know any more than he already did about this child, who'd somehow claimed a piece of his heart before ever being born.

"Ryan?"

He looked at her then. "What are you having, Anna?"

"A girl. Her name is Ruby. After Mateo's grandmother."

He gulped past the lump in his throat. "Ruby Reyes will be as beautiful as her mom."

Anna blushed. "I'll meet her in less than a month."

But not him. He still planned to leave right after Christmas.

He picked up a lullaby CD. "Better get this, too. For when Ruby's favorite baritone isn't around."

For a moment, Anna looked exactly the way he felt lately every time he pictured his leave-taking. She took the CD from him and turned away.

"What about a bassinet, Anna?"

Her shoulders tensed. "I'll save my money for a crib. Charlie and Evy can help me pick one out later."

Ryan didn't want Charlie and Evy to pick out Ruby's crib. Ruby… He gritted his teeth. Exactly why he hadn't asked before.

Now he had a name to put to the little face he'd be missing when he was alone in the condo in North Carolina. But he wanted Ruby to have something from him. Otherwise, there'd be nothing to remind Ruby of the man who once—

Steeling himself against the rush of emotion, he pointed the cart toward the checkout counter. Good thing he'd already started a special project for Ruby.

"You ever going to decorate that sad excuse for a Christmas tree, Anna Banana?"

Anna's brown eyes narrowed as if sensing something amiss. She'd always been able to read him. "You up for some tree trimming soon?"

He got in the checkout line. "Just say the word. I can trim with the best of 'em. Trim like nobody's business."

She emptied the cart of the smaller items. "Want to ride to church later for the costume fitting?"

The cashier ran the items through the scanner. Keeping an eye on the digital display, he lifted the heavier items for the cashier to scan. "I can't this afternoon."

"Both of us need to be fitted—"

"The advantage of having a sister with a costume design degree is that she can do the fitting in the privacy of our home. And I have other plans."

"Other plans?" Anna's voice quieted. "Oh."

He loaded the baby stuff into his car. Climbing into the passenger seat, her mouth thinned. She glared at him when she caught him checking out the dashboard clock for the fourth time. His other plans involved the secret project he was working on for Ruby.

Ryan refused her offer to help unload the trunk. "It'll be quicker if I do it myself."

Lifting her chin, she held the door for him. With quick efficiency, he stacked the purchases in a spare bedroom.

He wiped his hands against his jeans. "That about does it."

"Well, then." She made a sweeping gesture. "Don't let me keep you from your *other* plans."

He paused at the front door. "Are you feeling okay, Anna?"

She bared her teeth. "Never better."

His eyebrows rose. Must be pregnancy hormones.

Not for the first time, he was thankful to be a guy.

Ryan drove home. Later in the woodworking shop behind the barn, he became so engrossed in his project—

"What's that?"

Jolting, he grabbed his chest. "Give a guy a warning next time, Tess."

"Is that a—? Oh, Ryan. It's gorgeous."

Ryan pulled a drop cloth to hide the evidence. "Were you needing something, sis?"

Tessa's large, doe eyes reminded him of Anna. "I can drop off the manger you made when I head to church for the costume fitting."

He scrubbed his jaw. "Thanks. Let me carry it out for you."

Ryan steered Tessa to the opposite side of the shed, where he'd stored the rough-hewn manger. He hadn't expected anyone to walk into his private domain. Since Dad died, the shop had become a place to work with his hands.

Cutting. Drilling. Sanding. Amid the aromatic scents of fresh-cut lumber, a place to quiet his thoughts. A place to pray about the yearnings of his heart. Which, until recently, he'd believed fulfilled when he accepted the new research job.

Now he wasn't so sure. Contentment with his leave-taking was not the primary emotion he was feeling. He lifted the feeding trough in his arms.

Outside the barn, sunlight shimmered off Tessa's brown curls. She surged ahead to her blue Camry. "Ethan's got the hay bale in the trunk. I hope the manger will fit on the seat."

He shifted the weight in his arms. "Maybe I should go with you and put this in the gazebo."

She flexed her biceps. "Farm Girl has this under control."

He regretted what family responsibilities had cost his youngest sister. As the oldest, he should've done something to make sure she didn't have to give up her dreams, too. Never one to complain, Tessa had given up her plans to work on a Broadway production.

"I'll miss you, Tess." But for the first time, he acknowledged to himself that what he was giving up might be more than he'd gain.

Perennially bubbly, her mouth drooped. "Are you sure this job is what you really want?"

He dropped his gaze. "I've been working toward this goal ever since I returned home."

"It's okay for dreams to change, though. If that's what you want."

He placed the manger on the seat. "Who said my dream has changed?"

"Then what's with the cradle?" She motioned toward the shop. "And if you're leaving, do you think it's wise to spend so much time with Anna?"

His little sister was giving him life advice? "I don't expect you to understand, Tess. It's just something I have to do. To be there for her as a friend."

"But is friendship all you're feeling for her?" Tessa folded her arms. "Are you being honest with yourself? I want you to be happy, Ryan."

Ryan closed the door with a soft click. "I am happy, Tess. Ecstatic at the thought of a brand-new life."

His brand-new, lonely life. He winced. Maybe he wasn't as excited as he'd been a month ago.

She circled to the driver side. "I just don't want you to deny yourself the possibility of more."

He shuffled his feet. "Anna has made it clear that we're friends. Nothing more. And I'm fine with that."

"Are you sure?" Tessa looked at him across the car roof. "We love you, Ryan. You sacrificed so much to keep Dad's dream alive. We just want to make sure you don't lose yours."

"I am sure." His voice clogged. "And the family's support means more than you could ever know."

"I'm going to have to ask you—*again*—to hold still." The words were as sharp as the pins in Tessa Savage's mouth.

Startled, Anna glanced downward.

On her hands and knees in the fellowship hall of the church, Tessa secured the hemline with a couple of pins. She made a circling motion with her hand. Her arms at right angles, Anna did a half-turn rotation on the small dais.

A frown marred the usually untroubled serenity of Ryan's youngest sister. Tessa had been about Oscar's age when Anna left for college.

"I look that bad, huh?"

Tessa rose. "I've made the necessary adjustments so the loose-fitting style accommodates the wide load of your extra bulk."

Anna blinked. Wide load? Bulk? That stung sharper than any of the steel pins stuck into the pincushion strapped to Tessa's wrist.

"Is something wrong, Tess?"

Tessa smoothed a fold in the simple muslin shift. Reaching over, she draped the ends of the azure blue veil over Anna's shoulders. "With your olive skin tone and eyes, you look like you could be the mother of Jesus."

"Great. As long as I don't have to do anything but sit. Speaking of sitting?" She took a wobbly step off the platform.

Tessa steadied her arm.

"What's wrong?" Anna squeezed her hand. "If there's anything—"

"Please don't hurt my brother." She clung to Anna. "He's so confused right now."

"What're you talking about?" Anna placed her hand atop her belly. "Ryan is the one leaving me."

Tessa's eyes widened.

Anna's heart pounded. "I mean..."

He wasn't leaving her. That implied a relationship far more than friendship. Ryan was leaving many things— teaching, the kids, the farm, his friends and family. But he was most certainly, most definitely *not* leaving her. Right?

Tessa gripped her arm. "If that's how you really feel, you should tell him."

"It doesn't matter what I feel." Anna frowned. "I won't

be the one to stand between Ryan and his dream, Tess. It has to be his choice."

Tessa's eyes welled. "Please don't tell Ryan I said anything. I'm just afraid he's making a mistake in leaving."

She took Tessa's hand in hers. "He's your brother. I'd do the same if I was afraid for Ben or Will." She sank onto the cushioned stool. "But it's complicated. Both of us have experienced loss."

"Both of you are scared." Tessa raised her chin. "But Ryan comes alive with those students, and since you've been home I've never seen him so happy."

Anna took a shuddering breath. Tessa hit too close to a truth she wasn't ready to examine. "The baby has to be my first priority. And Ryan has to decide what he wants for himself."

"Are you sure you're okay to drive home?" Tessa gnawed her lower lip. "I'm supposed to fit the shepherds next, but…"

"I'm fine." She waved Tessa away. "Go ahead."

After changing her clothes, Anna exited the church. Across the square, a customer emerged from the florist shop. Giving in to an urge she'd not been able to quell since meeting Kristina at the garden center, she crossed the street to admire the display window.

Kristina Collier had re-created the fishing hamlet of Kiptohanock in miniature. But unlike the real-time version of the coastal town, she'd daubed the buildings and square in fake snow.

Lights glowed through tiny stained glass windows at the church. And wee lanterns illuminated the green. Diminutive wreaths decked the doors of the model library, cafe and florist shop. Minuscule fire engines rested in the open bay of the station. Small Coast Guard and American flags hung outside the pint-size boat station.

Anna glanced up as the bell to the florist shop jingled. The door opened and closed behind Kristina with a whoosh. Kristina touched her fingertip to the window. "Beyond the edge of the square, if you use your imagination, you can almost see the Pruitt house."

In the glass reflection, Anna's gaze darted to the blonde florist.

She adjusted the strap of her purse on her shoulder. "Wishful thinking or do you know something the forecasters don't?"

Kristina wrapped the long ends of her taupe cardigan around herself. "If nothing else, one can dream." Her smile was bright. "How's motherhood treating you, Anna?"

"Dreams are a funny thing… Having the baby is more wonderful than I could ever imagine. Yet there are consequences I hadn't envisioned when I embarked on this journey to carry Mateo's baby." Anna gulped. "Alone."

"Is there something I can do for you, Anna? And I'm not talking about flowers."

Anna bit her lip. "How long were you a widow before you found love again?"

Kristina's eyes met hers in the mirrored reflection. "Or do you mean, how long before I *allowed* myself to love again?"

Anna sighed. "That, too."

"Canyon says he loved me almost immediately. But I was consumed with keeping Pax's memory alive. And single-parenting my son."

Anna chewed on her bottom lip. Spending time with Ryan again after so many years, she'd never imagined the feelings he'd awaken inside her.

Kristina placed a gentle hand on her own butterball-size stomach. A primal gesture. "I'm guessing you can understand better than most how I felt, Anna. Lonely yet determined to protect my heart."

Anna closed her eyes, shutting out the present. Replaying the final Christmas she shared with Mateo. And the next Christmas after his death when she discovered the IVF treatment had failed again.

She'd been so focused on conceiving and then so grateful for her baby, she never envisioned anything more in her life.

"Military widows go through the fire, Anna. And no one comes through a fire unscathed." Kristina's voice quavered. "Only when I nearly lost Canyon to an actual forest fire did I realize life is for the living. For my child's sake— but mostly for my own—I had to embrace the beautiful gift God was giving me in Canyon's love."

Anna shook her head. "I'm stuck between what was and what may never be."

"I'll always love Pax." A faraway look entered Kristina's eyes. "But I love Canyon, too. And if you truly want to embrace a new life, you have to let go of the past."

Anna threw out her hands. "I don't deserve a new life. It's my fault Ruby will never know her father."

Kristina touched Anna's shoulder. "Why do you think it's your fault?"

"It's my fault Mateo never held a child in his arms." Tears streamed down Anna's cheeks. "We had so little time together. I told him we were perfect the way we were. I didn't want to be a military mom."

"That's nothing to be ashamed of, Anna. It's a tremendous responsibility, which isn't right for every woman."

Anna's gaze skimmed over the green. "I told him we didn't need anyone else."

Kristina took Anna's hand. "You didn't know what was

coming. You were following your instincts about what was right for you at the time."

"What about what was right for Mateo?" Anna raised her tearstained face. "Every time he mentioned having a baby, I put him off."

Kristina pressed her hand. "You need to forgive yourself, Anna. Give yourself a break."

Anna swiped at her cheeks with the back of her hand. "I thought we had plenty of time."

"I don't believe he'd want you to spend the rest of your life alone. He'd want you and the baby to have the fullest life possible. To savor every gift the Lord has for you."

"But I don't deserve a second chance, not after I caused Mateo to lose his."

"Don't make this child your penance, Anna. Choosing aloneness for the wrong reason only dishonors who he was and what you were to each other."

She pinched her lips together. "I hadn't considered it that way before."

"Do you believe in God, Anna?"

Her eyes flicked to Kristina. "Yes, I do."

"Then believe He's always been in control. That He is in control now. No matter our mistakes—what we did or didn't do—He can make everything work for good."

Did she believe God was in control when Mateo died? Or during the pain of infertility? Was He working things out for her even now?

Certainty gripped Anna. He'd brought her home to Kiptohanock, hadn't He? She scanned the village. Places familiar and dear to her.

Although she didn't understand the whys of her life, she recognized God had everything under control. And somehow—she didn't know the how yet—God would work everything for her and Ruby's ultimate good.

"It's k-kind of a lot to take in." Anna's voice wobbled.

Kristina hugged her. "God is like that. Bigger than we can imagine. Far more than we can comprehend." She stepped back. "But His ways are always for His children."

A woman headed toward the florist shop.

"Looks like you have another customer." Anna breathed deeply of the briny, seaside air. "Thanks for everything."

Kristina smiled. "See you at the cookie swap next weekend?"

"Do I look like I need cookies?" She patted her abdomen. "But I'll be there. Wouldn't miss it for the world."

As for Ryan? How did her changing feelings for him fit into what God was doing? Or was she on the brink of another mistake? Was their relationship a disaster in the making?

Chapter Eleven

Between baby-stuff expeditions and working on the cradle, thoughts of Zander dogged Ryan's thoughts all weekend. It was late on Sunday when Ryan had the brilliant idea to contact Zander's bus driver, who had to know where he picked up and dropped off the child every day.

In a place like the Shore where everybody knew somebody who knew everybody else, he finally managed to get the bus driver's number. And learned that Zander lived in public housing. A drug-infested, crime-ridden neighborhood the tourists never saw. A pocket of rural poverty and multigenerational despair.

Many of the residents, like Zander's family, had once been migrant workers at one of the large agribusinesses. And at some point, found year-round work on the Shore.

"The grandma used to wait at the bus stop for him," Bennie Hollingsworth said over the phone. "She's a Haitian lady. But I don't see her anymore. And if anybody's there at all to meet him, it's the uncle." Bennie's voice altered. "That guy's kind of scary."

Ryan's gut knotted.

"Poor kid. Not much chance of a better future." Bennie

sighed. "I heard his mom is serving time for drug possession with intent to sell."

His spirits sank further.

"Mr. Savage? If you don't mind me saying so, I don't think it would be a good idea to pay the Benoits a visit tonight. It's already dark, and you're an outsider. Even in daylight, don't go without law enforcement."

So first thing Monday morning, Ryan waited at the bus lane at school, anxious to touch base with Zander. To find out why he didn't show on Friday. But most of all, to make sure the little guy was okay.

And if Zander didn't make it to school, Ryan had a substitute on standby so he could go look for him. But to Ryan's immense relief, the child in his ragged jacket stepped off the bus. "Zander, my man."

The little boy's head snapped up. But the scowl etched on his forehead eased a fraction at the sight of Ryan waiting for him.

"We missed you at the tree lighting." Ryan looked him over. "Did something come up?"

His heart sank at the flash of belligerence in Zander's eyes. "I ain't got time for baby stuff like that. I had to take care of my grandma." His chin wobbled momentarily before resuming its rock hard appearance. "My uncle needed my help."

"It wasn't the same without you."

Zander snorted. "Yeah, right."

"I mean it."

"People say a lot of things." Zander's lip curled. "Save it for somebody who needs that baby stuff. Can I go now?"

Ryan moved aside as the third grader stomped inside the building. He had a bad feeling about the boy. The child was like a time bomb waiting to blow. All that was needed was the match. Maybe only a spark. And then kaboom.

He shook his head as he headed toward his fifth-grade classroom. Ryan had foolishly believed he and Zander had reached an understanding. Maybe he wasn't cut out for this mentoring thing.

Zander's problems were beyond the scope of his ability to solve. Someone else would have to take up where Ryan left off. Someone smarter and more savvy.

The morning flew by for Ryan. And then it was time for his favorite portion of the day—science.

He pointed to the word he'd written on the whiteboard. "A mixture is a combo of two or more substances that do not lose their characteristics when combined."

At the sound of restless bodies, he faced the class. "Can anyone think of an example of a mixture in real life?"

He could have heard a pin drop in the sudden, profound silence. There were surreptitious glances at the wall clock. Only a few minutes remained until lunch. A kid's stomach growled.

"Anyone?"

He could think of a perfect example from real life. His life. Teachers had to be a unique mixture—one part entertainer, one part counselor and one part air traffic controller.

A glazed look had overtaken the features of his students. Flashing like a neon sign—starvation imminent. They were fading fast. He'd better do something quick or lose their attention for good.

"No one can name even one example of a mixture?" Pretending disappointment, he propped his hands on his hips. "Well, if no one knows the answer, then don't plan on leaving the classroom for lunch."

There were round-eyed stares and gasps of horror. But now for the surprise.

"Okay, write this down. Here's an example of a mixture from everyday life." Walking across the classroom, he yanked open the door and took the three pizza boxes out of the arms of the delivery boy. "Pizza anyone?"

The room went slightly wild.

"Is that for us, Mr. Savage?"

"What kind is it, Mr. Savage?"

He smiled. "Yes. Yes. And pepperoni." He turned to the delivery boy. "What do I owe you?"

"You're set, Mr. Savage." The delivery guy patted his uniform shirt. "I got the money from the secretary at the front office."

He waited until everyone was about to bring a slice to their mouths when—

"But wait!" He smacked his hand to his forehead. "What was I thinking? We can't eat pizza."

Someone groaned.

"We can't eat pizza without something to drink, too." He cocked his head. "Does anyone have a *solution*?"

Quick grins. By now, the kids were beginning to catch on to his game. They studied solutions yesterday.

The Evans kid raised his hand. "What we need, Mr. Savage, is something liquid. Where a solute has dissolved into another substance called the solvent." He waggled his eyebrows. "Which together become a solution."

Ryan fingered his chin. "Anybody have an example of this solution thingy Evans mentioned?"

"Please…" Max Scott slumped in his chair. "Somebody? Anybody? The pizza's getting cold."

Everyone laughed. Izzie Clark raised her hand. "Like lemonade, Mr. Savage?"

He pretended to consider her suggestion. "That might work. Or would this do?" He whipped out a pitcher of cherry Kool-Aid from the supply closet. There were cheers.

"Finally…" Max moaned. "Somebody pass out the cups before he decides to go into the next unit."

"Actually, there was one other example I thought of… A great example of a mixture. And something to enjoy watching while we eat."

He plucked the towel off the small bowl on his desk. "A goldfish in a bowl."

There were gasps and a buzz of excitement. He loved to see the joy of learning light their eyes.

He'd put off telling them that he wasn't coming back after winter break. He was going to miss them. But he had to make his announcement soon. His chest tightened. The final days before winter break were ticking down.

And yet again, doubts clouded the goal he'd set for himself—to be in the lab come January. Was he doing the right thing in walking away from teaching? Walking away from his kids?

Walking away from Anna? He squared his shoulders. He couldn't turn back the clock on either his job or Anna.

The fifth-grade classroom now belonged to the new guy in the process of moving to the Shore to take Ryan's place. As for Anna?

She'd never belonged to him. The pressure inside his chest intensified. And she never would.

Everyone had settled down to inhaling lunch when a knock sounded on the door, and Principal Carden strode into the classroom. "Mr. Savage, I'm afraid I need your help with a situation."

"Of course, sir."

Mr. Carden motioned. "I've asked Mrs. Murphy to take over until you return." The guidance counselor stepped inside the room.

Ryan glanced at the sea of faces, who never missed a trick. "I expect a good report when I return. Mrs. Murphy?" He picked a sheaf of papers off his desk. "My lesson plan for after lunch."

Principal Carden gently closed the door behind them. "Sorry to disrupt your class, Ryan, but we had a situation erupt in the lunchroom a few minutes ago."

"Sure. Okay. What's up?"

But Mr. Carden walked past the cafeteria. "It's Zander Benoit."

Ryan slumped. "What did he do?"

"Apparently, there was an altercation in the lunchroom with another student. Zander decked the kid and laid him out on the floor." Mr. Carden shook his head. "Then Zander took off."

Ryan's mouth thinned. "Where is he? Is he hurt?"

"He fled to the media center. And since you've developed a rapport with him…" Mr. Carden frowned. "Zander's under one of the tables and refuses to come out."

"I'll talk to him, see if I can get him to de-escalate."

"This is the final straw for him, Ryan. I hoped the after-school program would help us to avoid taking a more drastic step. But if he can't get his anger and aggression under control, we're going to have to remove him from the regular classroom."

Ryan clenched his jaw. For Zander, placing him in a self-contained class for kids with emotional and behavioral problems would be the equivalent of writing him off. The kid had so much potential.

Mr. Carden stepped away as Anna hurried toward him.

"I'm so glad I caught you. The kindergarten aide took my class." She panted for breath. "I wanted to make sure you knew. I saw everything in the cafeteria. It wasn't Zander's fault. The other kid started the fight."

He scrubbed the back of his neck. "It doesn't matter who started the fight. Zander shouldn't have reacted the way he did." Discouragement swirled in his gut. "I believed we were finally getting through to him."

She touched Ryan's arm. "I think you *are* getting through to him. I talked to Zander's teacher. The other kid had been ragging Zander. He made sure everyone knew Zander's mom was in prison."

Ryan sighed.

She raised her chin. "The kid called Zander a stupid loser from a stupid family who weren't smart enough to not get nabbed by the police."

Ryan closed his eyes. "Poor little guy."

"What will you say to him?"

Ryan opened his eyes. "I have no idea."

Anna squeezed his hand. "I'm praying for you as you talk to him. For wisdom."

He stared at her hand and gently pulled away. "Thanks. I need all the help I can get." The no-touch policy wasn't working as well as he'd hoped. But now was not the time to dwell on that.

Inside the media center, Ryan paused to pray for Zander and himself. That somehow God would give him the words he needed to get through to the third grader.

Since meeting Zander, he'd done some online research about children with behavioral issues. The experts advised caring, supportive adults to concentrate on building rapport. And when an incident erupted, to work with the child on identifying the problem or trigger. Easier said than done.

He found Zander underneath the table where they usually worked together on math. Careful to respect Zander's personal space, he took a deep breath and crouched down. "Zan, my man."

The child looked up, his black lashes spiky with tears. The fear, pain and rage in the eight-year-old's gaze was like a punch in Ryan's gut.

"I heard what happened."

Zander's face scrunched. "So they sent you to kick my butt out the door?" His eyes welled, and he studied the carpet.

"I totally get why you freaked, man. I wanted to do the same thing when my dad died. I was so angry. And mixed up. And sad."

Zander scuffed the carpet with his shoe.

"I had to leave my girlfriend, my job and my apartment because my family needed me to come home and help. But now, I'm sorry for the way I acted."

Zander didn't say anything, but Ryan had his attention.

"Although it seemed horrible at the time, it brought me back to Kiptohanock. Where I had the chance to meet you. And I wouldn't trade the last few years here at school for anything."

Ryan blinked. He'd not expected that to come out of his mouth.

Zander's eyes narrowed. "Fo' real?"

"For real. But I get you being mad." He extended his hands in front of him, inches apart. "So how angry do you really feel? This much?" He opened his arms wider. "Or this much?"

Zander shook his head and spread his arms as wide as the space allowed. "This much."

Ryan gestured. "Mind if I join you?"

Zander made an elaborate shrug. "Knock yourself out, Mr. Savage."

Getting on his knees, Ryan crawled inside and banged his head on the underside of the table. "Ow!"

Zander grinned.

"I live to amuse you kids." Ryan gave him a sheepish grin. "Dudes like us, sometimes we get mad."

Zander made a face. "'Cause people like Brandon are idiots."

"Question is—when people say and do things that hurt us—how can we avoid going ballistic?" Ryan cocked his head. "And avoid suspension."

Zander scowled. "I don't know."

Step Two—replacing inappropriate behavior with a better coping strategy. And Ryan suddenly remembered reading an article about energy therapy with troubled children.

"This is going to sound insane, man, but just do what I'm doing." Ryan tapped the tip of his nose with his index finger in a steady rhythm. 1-2-3-4. 1-2-3-4.

Zander's gaze went wide. "That's stupid, Mr. Savage."

Ryan raised his eyebrow. *"Stupid?"*

Zander flushed. "Not stupid. Sorry."

"Try it. Maybe not on your nose, but somewhere else on your body. Whatcha got to lose?"

Zander narrowed his eyes, but tapped his finger on his forehead. 1-2-3-4. 1-2-3-4.

Ryan decided to mix it up. He transferred the beat to his chest. And changed the rhythm.

Tongue rolling in his cheek, Zander matched him beat for beat. Ryan beat out a complex rhythm from one of his favorite jazz tunes.

Copying the rhythm, Zander laughed out loud. And head bobbing, he thrust out his skinny chest, switching the beat to a complicated hip-hop rap.

Ryan threw out his hands in surrender. "How much anger are you feeling now, Zan?"

Zander held his hands only a few inches apart.

Step Three—create an action plan. "So next time somebody mouths off, instead of whacking 'em…?" He held his breath.

Zander pursed his lips. "Do the tapping thing?"

Ryan pretended to consider it. "That's workable. If

you're willing to do it instead of flipping out because you're mad."

Step Four—reinforce the commitment to the plan by letting the child own the behavior and the solution.

"Okay."

Ryan smiled. "I'll let your teacher and Principal Carden know about the plan you've made."

Zander scooted out from underneath the table and waited for Ryan, whose older knee joints took longer to clear the table. Getting to his feet, he was surprised when Zander threw his arms around his waist.

"Thanks, Mr. Savage. You're the smartest, best teacher in the whole world. It's going to be the greatest year ever."

His eyelids burned as he returned Zander's hug. How would Zander react when he learned Ryan was leaving? The pressure inside his chest increased dramatically. Would Zander regress and act out again if Ryan wasn't there to support him?

The struggle between fulfilling his career goals and the call of his heart nearly split Ryan in two.

Chapter Twelve

A few days later, Mr. Carden caught Anna on her way to the after-school program. "A moment, Mrs. Reyes?"

Teacher or not, a visit by the principal provoked anxiety. She racked her brain for anything she'd done to deserve a reprimand. One week before break, surely he hadn't come to fire her?

She needed this job and the paycheck for every day remaining on her interim contract. As to what she'd be doing after Ruby was born? She sighed. One obstacle at a time. God would provide as He always had.

Mr. Carden's expression softened. "Nothing to worry about, Mrs. Reyes. On the contrary. I think I have good news for you."

Good news she could use.

He smiled. "I've received nothing but glowing reports regarding your performance here."

"Thank you, Mr. Carden. I hope you will consider including that in my personnel file."

"Of course, I'd be happy to provide any references you require, but I hope it won't be necessary."

She frowned. "I don't understand."

"Mrs. Thompson telephoned today."

Her mouth went dry. Was Mrs. Thompson returning from maternity leave early?

"She's decided to remain at home with her baby for the rest of the school year. And I'd like to offer you the teaching position on a semi-permanent basis." He inclined his head. "After you finish your own maternity leave, of course."

Anna stared, not sure she'd heard him correctly. "For the rest of the year?"

"I can't promise the same kindergarten position next year, but I'm pretty confident I'll have a position for you in the fall, too."

Thank You, God.

She threw her arms around the slightly rotund principal. His eyes bulged as her belly bumped into him. She let go. "Oh, I'm sorry."

But Mr. Carden smiled as he straightened his tie. "I am delighted we will have you on board."

That night, she and Ryan decorated her Christmas tree with handmade ornaments her kindergarten class made for her. It was maybe the best Christmas tree ever. Even Ryan gave his grudging approval.

When she told him about her news, he congratulated her. But there was something in his eyes she couldn't decipher. Regret?

"Everything's working out for you." He glanced around the trailer. "And I hope as soon as your budget allows, you'll find a better place to live, closer to town."

She threw him a grin, hoping to make him smile. "And aren't you thrilled you won't be around to haul the boxes?"

He didn't smile. "There is that."

Anna's smile faded. What had she wanted him to say? But she knew. She wanted him to say that once he took the new job off-Shore, he'd miss her as much as she'd miss him.

She tried again. "I guess you've started packing."

He shrugged. "I'll get to it." And adjusted one of the seashell ornaments on the tree.

"Aren't you eager to shake the Kiptohanock sand off your feet for bigger and better things?"

He shrugged. "Kiptohanock has a lot to recommend it, too."

She tilted her head. "Like me."

He exhaled. "It will be hard to say goodbye to my students." Still he didn't look at her. "It'll be hard to say goodbye to a lot of things."

"Like what?"

Ryan fiddled with one of the tiny bows on a branch of the Christmas tree. "Zander. Maria. Oscar, of course…"

Her frustration mounted. What about missing her? But she wouldn't put words in his mouth. Maybe he'd be relieved to get away from her projects.

"No more farm chores, though. Getting your own space back. From now on, you'll have a real lunch hour. And—"

"Lunch duty isn't so bad."

"But," she prodded, "you'll be getting your old life back. Which is what you want, right?"

"How do you envision your future, Anna? Beyond diapers, I mean."

This time, her gaze slid away from the penetrating look in his eyes. "Is there life beyond diapers?" She laughed.

He didn't. Instead, he reached for his coat. "Only you can answer that question, Anna."

"I don't know what you mean."

His eyes bored into hers. "I think you do." He raked his hand over his head. "Or maybe it's already too late.

Perhaps there are no second chances, Anna." Pivoting, he walked out of the trailer.

Was that true? As he drove away, she sank into the armchair. Is that how Ryan viewed the future? Too late for a second chance. Did that include their relationship, too?

The next day the guidance counselor paged Ryan to her office. And he had a feeling Zander was somehow involved. He practically ran to the front office, expecting the worst.

He'd been spending a lot of time after school since the breakthrough last week with Zander. His grades had risen dramatically, and they'd made so much progress together. What had happened? Was this the straw that would mean suspension or an alternative classroom for Zander?

The counselor met Ryan at the door. Zander sat in one of the chairs. Tapping a beat on the wooden arm.

"One of the other kids called Zander names." The counselor patted the child's back. "But instead of punching him, Zander went to his teacher and started tapping."

Never losing the beat, Zander whispered under his breath, "I am a good kid, and I deserve respect. I am a good kid, and I deserve respect."

Ryan's throat constricted. "You are a good kid, Zander."

Zander stopped tapping and grinned. "I felt myself getting mad, but I remembered to tap, Mr. Savage. And I didn't explode."

"I'm so proud of you, Zander." He gripped Zander's shoulder. "Keep up the good work."

"You helped me, Mr. Savage. Thanks." Zander's face was alight with pride at controlling his temper.

Ryan's chest tightened. He'd somehow managed to make a difference in Zander's life, finding a way to stem the downward spiral.

More than anything, he dreaded telling Zander goodbye. Would Zander be okay? Would another adult step forward to fill the gap in Zander's life?

Poking his head around the doorframe, Mr. Carden called Ryan into his office. The principal made him an offer he hadn't expected. A chance to oversee the at-risk student program. A chance to stay with his kids. A chance to pursue a future with Anna.

If that's what he wanted. Did he? Was he willing to put his heart out there again? Had he been wrong about second chances?

Saturday morning in the Pruitt kitchen, Anna placed the last of the cookies she'd made on the platter.

Evy handed her the green cellophane. "What are those called?"

She held the box while Evy rolled out a section of cellophane along the serrated edge. *"Polvorones."*

Evy stretched the plastic wrap over the platter. "Say that three times fast."

Anna laughed. "Otherwise known as Mexican wedding cookies. Mateo's grandmother made these when we were restationed to Texas."

Evy secured the wrap around the tray. "They look like yummy powdered sugar snowballs to me."

Anna glanced out the kitchen window. "Maybe the closest to snow we're likely to get this Christmas."

Evy placed Anna's platter in a large cardboard box to transport the goodies to the Duer inn.

Anna's tummy rumbled. "Baby Reyes can't wait to sample one of her Aunt Evy's Chinese almond cookies."

Evy fluttered her lashes. "Baby Reyes must take after her Uncle Charlie. I had to threaten him to keep his hands off, or I wouldn't have enough for the cookie swap."

"Poor Charlie. My brother has always loved cookies."

"No need to feel sorry for Charlie." Evy grabbed her coat draped across the island stool. "I made him an extra batch. Which he'll discover when he starts roaming the kitchen looking for a snack."

She gave Evy full kudos for managing to keep her youngest, headstrong brother in check. Had to be love. Anna refused to give in to the sigh she was feeling about her own prospects for love.

Instead, she shifted her attention to the sound of the television in the family room. "Thanks for encouraging Charlie to invite Ryan to watch a game while we're at the party."

She shrugged into her coat. Decorating the tree last night, Ryan had been in a strange mood. She reached for the box on the counter.

"I'll get this." Evy hefted the box in her arms. "After our book club holiday social, Charlie needs some male bonding time."

Anna rolled her tongue inside her cheek. "What book was it this quarter?"

Her burly brother—football star and tough law enforcement officer—attending a weekly book club with a bunch of women boggled her mind.

"Anna Karenina."

Deputy Sheriff Charlie Pruitt—classic Russian literature reader? Love certainly did make the world go round.

"Bye, Charlie," Evy called.

A grunt from the living room.

"Men," Evy huffed, but a smile played about her lips.

Anna held the door. "Mom and I were outnumbered five to two. You have no idea how long we've waited for another female to balance the numbers." She studied Evy's Mini Cooper.

Evy settled the box in the back seat. "What's wrong?"

"Just wondering if I'll fit."

Evy wrenched open the driver door. "You and your baby bump are gorgeous."

Anna shoehorned herself into the passenger seat. "You're the one who's going to have to pry me out with a crowbar."

Evy helped Anna click the seat belt in place. "See? Not too big. Not too small. Just right."

"Thank you, Goldilocks." Anna gazed at her blonde sister-in-law with affection. "It's a snug fit."

Evy negotiated the village square, which emptied north on Seaside Road. As the isolated farmhouses and woodland on each side of the road flew past, Anna adjusted the seat belt over her stomach. Soon Evy turned onto the oyster-shelled drive of the inn.

And Anna got her first look at the longtime Duer family home, refurbished after a devastating hurricane a few years ago.

The wraparound porch of the three-story Victorian twinkled with strands of white lights. From inside, an enormous Christmas tree glowed. Evy parked among the other vehicles.

"Looks like the whole town is here."

"The female population leastways." Evy slid out. "Honey loves entertaining. The more, the merrier."

Anna did her best to extricate herself from the Mini Cooper. Graceful at eight months pregnant, she was not. Evy's brother, Sawyer, met them on the porch steps.

"Going somewhere, big brother?"

Sawyer took the box from Evy. They'd been separated by the foster system as children and had only reunited a year ago. "I'm getting out while the getting is good. After I put this box of yours in the dining room."

Inside the inn, they were immediately surrounded by Kiptohanock merrymakers. The broad-shouldered ex-Coastie disappeared in the direction of the dining room. Honey—the Eastern Shore's own Martha Stewart—had outfitted the inn with a beach chic decor. Whitened beach driftwood and sea glass sculptures bedecked side tables.

With Evy enveloped by Margaret Davenport, Anna found herself admiring the blue spruce in the bay window.

"A Savage Farm tree." Honey joined her. "Merry Christmas, Anna."

She hugged Honey.

"Look at you." Honey touched a light hand to Anna's bump. "So radiant."

"As you must've been last year, pregnant with baby Daisy."

Honey squeezed Anna's hand. "I was a hot mess of swelled ankles and aching back. But Sawyer and I wouldn't trade one minute with Daisy." She made a wry grimace. "Once we got past the six months of no sleep."

Not for the first time, Anna wondered how she'd manage to teach full-time and parent a newborn alone. Lots of women did it, though. She'd do what she had to do.

"Speaking of sweethearts—baby and cowboy..." Honey's eyes flitted toward Sawyer, holding their daughter in his arms. Just turned one, Daisy had blond hair very like her Aunt Evy's.

Father and daughter didn't make it far. Every woman from seventeen-year-old Jade Collier to ninety-year-old Mrs. Evans appeared duty bound to greet the baby. Good-natured, Sawyer grinned and adjusted the bulging diaper bag over his shoulder.

"Where're they off to?"

Honey smiled. "To watch the game with Charlie and the other spouses of the women here at the inn."

"Not so much fun for Daisy."

Honey waved as Daisy blew her a kiss. "Amelia's preschooler Patrick will be there. Besides, Daisy will enjoy wrapping the guys around her little finger."

Anna bit the inside of her cheek.

Honey's brown eyes sparkled. "Apples don't fall far from trees." She nudged Anna. "And Daisy's Uncle Charlie is the biggest marshmallow of all."

Anna laughed. "He and Evy are going to be wonderful parents someday."

Honey smiled. "I'm so happy your daughter will grow up here with her cousin Daisy."

Cousins. In the endearing, quirky and totally Southern way of counting kinfolk. Even those only related by marriage. And for the moment, Anna forgot to feel so alone.

Her throat tightened, imagining future Christmases with the Pruitt clan. Thanksgiving and Easter. Fourth of July parades. Her church family.

Picnics on the barrier island beaches in summer, hunting for sea glass. A dark-haired little girl with rosebud lips, herself and the laughing, blue-green eyes of—

Her heart stutter-stepped. What was she doing? None of that was meant to be. Ryan had another life waiting for him. A life without her or Ruby. It was better for everyone this way.

Wasn't it?

Honey moved to the center of the room. "Ladies? Your attention, please?"

The buzz of conversation diminished. Honey welcomed them to the cookie swap and laid out the party rules. "I hope everyone remembered to bring an empty container."

Standing beside the hand-carved mantel topped with toy sailboats, Evy gave Anna a thumbs-up.

Honey continued with the instructions. "First, choose

only a dozen. We'll go around again until the cookies are gone." She smoothed her green Christmas blouse. "I don't want any cookies left here."

Anna promised herself next year... Next year she'd have a baby *and* her slim figure again. She sighed. At least she'd have the baby.

In shades of shimmering turquoise and silver, the dining room was decorated as amazingly as the rest of the inn. Container in hand, Anna followed the ladies around the table.

The *polvorones* were nearly gone. Across the table, Justine smiled as Anna selected a Christmas wreath cookie from the Savage family kitchen. Anna also took an iced lighthouse cookie, created by Caroline Duer Clark.

"I had lots of artistic assistance." Caroline smiled fondly in the direction of her stepdaughter. But her expression turned wistful.

Though it was obvious Caroline adored Izzie, Anna knew firsthand how hard it was year after year to behold others' joy and yet have empty arms aching for a baby of your own. With a history of chronic depression, Caroline didn't want to risk passing on the genetic predisposition to a child.

Sandpiper Cafe waitress Dixie's contribution consisted of gingerbread starfish, dusted with cinnamon and begging to be devoured. But Honey had promised real food once the cookies were cleared off the table.

Evy took both their cookie-filled containers out to the car so Anna could have her hands free to munch. Honey insisted Anna take the comfy, butter-yellow armchair near the blazing hearth.

Anna no sooner settled into the cushion than the rest of the ladies trooped into the living room. Laden with pastel pink packages, to her astonishment, they placed the gifts beside her chair.

Evy threw out her hands. "Surprise!"

Anna's mouth dropped open. "What's this?"

"You wouldn't let us schedule a baby shower for you at church." Darcy Parks whipped out a notepad and pen. "So we planned one during the cookie exchange at Honey's house."

"But you didn't have to …" She tried to get up, but with plate in hand she couldn't rise to her feet.

Taking Anna's plate, Margaret moved in front of the tree. "Ladies? Positions, please."

"But…"

Margaret patted Anna's shoulder. "Enjoy yourself, dear. And let your friends love on you and your baby."

Darcy and Evy ensconced themselves on either side of Anna. Evy handed Anna a package to unwrap while Darcy jotted the name of the giver and a description of the present. Jade Collier carried the gifts to display on a nearby Queen Anne table.

Starting on the pile of presents, Anna folded back tissue paper to reveal the beautiful baby gifts. Warm baby mittens and a ribbon-trimmed cap from Pauline Crockett. Next, an exquisite hand-smocked red velvet dress from Darcy's mom, Agnes.

"If she's anything like her mother, Ruby will be beautiful in red." Agnes smiled.

Then, several children's storybooks from Charlie and Evy. "I hope Ruby will visit often, and we can read a book together in the reading nook." Evy's eyes glistened. "Charlie claims I married him for that fabulous nook."

Everyone laughed.

The final gift was from old Mrs. Evans. The rectangular-shaped box lay heavy in Anna's lap. An unusual silence reigned as she removed the last of the packaging. She glanced at the sea of expectant faces. It wasn't like the chatty women to fall quiet.

"Go ahead." Kristina motioned. "See what you've got."

Anna lifted the lid. Inside lay a pair of tiny pink booties and matching crocheted sweater atop a lovely receiving blanket.

"Oh, Mrs. Evans…" Her throat clogged as she brushed the soft material against her cheek. "It's so beautiful. Thank you."

The old woman's gnarled hand rested upon the crook of a cane.

Anna examined the perfect stitches. "How were you ever able to make this?"

Mrs. Evans's fingers had become misshapen through decades of hard work and the arthritis of old age. But her blue eyes—like a pair of faded denim jeans—sparkled with life.

"I make a set for every baby." The elderly woman's gaze brushed the faces around the crowded room. "And I intend to go on doing so until the good Lord sees fit to take me home."

Anna—with Evy and Darcy's assistance—lumbered to her feet. She planted a kiss on the old woman's papery thin cheek. "Thank you, Mrs. Evans."

Her eyes blurred as she contemplated old friends like the Duer sisters and new friends like Kristina Collier. "Thank you all. I never expected—" Her voice hitched.

She'd never expected any of this. She'd done the right thing in coming home to raise her baby. And every time she wrapped her child against the cold, she'd also wrap herself in the memory of this day, these women and their love against the backdrop of an Eastern Shore Christmas.

Batting moisture from her eyes, Margaret cleared her throat. "Mark your calendars for the annual Living Nativity. Featuring our own mother-to-be, Anna, as the mother of Jesus…"

Evy smiled at Anna.

"…and Ryan Savage as the humble carpenter God chose to be the earthly father of His Son." Margaret's eyebrow arched. "It promises to be an event none of you will want to miss."

Margaret made it sound as if she and Ryan were a real couple. But what if they were? Anna's heart beat a trifle faster. *What if they were?*

The party dispersed as the women gathered their belongings. While Darcy and Evy boxed the gifts for transport, Anna donned her coat, feeling superfluous. No one would allow her to clean up.

Dixie waylaid her on the porch. "See you soon, little sugar." She kissed her own fingers and pressed them against Anna's abdomen.

Evy's heeled boots clattered across the wide-planked veranda. "All aboard!"

Dixie draped an arm around Anna's shoulders. "I know your mama wishes she could've been here for the baby shower. So I took lots of photos with my phone."

Anna's heart clanged like a fire alarm inside her chest.

Dixie gave Anna a hug. "And as your mama's best friend, I emailed the pictures right away to her in Germany."

Anna went still. For a second, she actually believed she might faint.

"How considerate of you, Dixie." Evy pulled Anna toward the steps. "But Anna has had enough excitement for one day."

Dixie waved. "Y'all have a great evening."

Panic bubbled inside Anna as Evy guided her down the steps.

"Bye now!" called Dixie.

Anna clutched her sister-in-law's arm. "Evy…"

"Bye, Dixie!" Evy hustled Anna across the path. "Hang on…" She tucked Anna into the car. Clutching the dashboard, Anna couldn't catch her breath.

Evy wheeled onto Seaside Road. "Are you going to be sick?"

"I…think…I'm…hyper—venti—lating."

"Do I need to stop?" Evy's gaze ping-ponged from the road to Anna. "Should I roll down the window?"

Anna placed her hand on her throat.

Evy frowned. "I'd tell you to put your head between your knees, but that's probably an anatomical impossibility for you right now."

Anna stopped hyperventilating and stared at the petite blonde, white-knuckling the steering wheel. "If I wasn't so panicked, I'd laugh."

Evy's shoulders eased a fraction. "If it's any consolation, Dixie meant well. She had no idea you haven't told your parents."

Anna rested her head against the seat. "I should've known better than to keep this news from them."

"It will be okay."

"No, it won't." Anna stared out the window. "When Mom sees those photos, she's going to have a conniption. Her only daughter, pregnant and unmarried. I can only imagine what she'll think."

"Let's talk to Charlie. He'll know what to do."

When they reached the Pruitt Victorian, Anna was relieved to see only Ryan's car parked beside the curb.

Inside, Charlie proved less than encouraging. "I knew this would happen." His lantern jaw tightened. "This is Kiptohanock after all."

Evy sighed. "You flush a toilet at one end…"

"…and the other end soon knows." Anna shook her head. "But what now?"

Ryan pushed his glasses farther along the bridge of his nose. "When all else fails, how about the truth?"

She glared at him. "Not helpful."

Charlie folded his arms. "He's right. Will and I told you from the beginning this wasn't a secret you could or should expect to keep. Why haven't you told them?"

She wrung her hands. "I just couldn't. They're so busy helping Jaxon get through the holidays. If I'd told them about the baby, they'd have been on the first plane home."

Charlie clenched his teeth. "Mom is going to be mortified that she's the last to know. Dad will be livid."

"What's worse is how hurt they'll be." Anna blinked away tears. "They'll feel betrayed that I didn't include them in this decision."

Ryan tilted his head. "So why didn't you?"

She trembled. "They'd already sacrificed so much for me. They took early retirement and practically lived in Texas with me during Mateo's last year. They wouldn't have understood why I felt I had to have this baby." She placed her hand over her stomach.

Charlie exhaled. "You can expect a phone call ASAP." He grimaced. "Me, too. Demanding to know why they had to hear about a new grandchild from Dixie. I better warn Will. He'll have a call waiting for him when he gets off shift."

"I'm sorry," she whispered. "I've made a mess of everything."

Evy hugged her. "I'll be praying for you. And for your conversation with your mom."

Anna gulped. "A conversation long overdue."

Charlie nodded. "But don't sell our parents short. I think they'll understand. Eventually."

She slumped against the chair railing.

Ryan stepped forward. "I'll run Anna home." He opened the door. "Can you help me transfer the gifts from Evy's car, Charlie?"

"You knew?" Anna jutted her hip. "Did everyone in Kiptohanock know about the surprise baby shower but me?"

Charlie rolled his eyes as he shouldered his way outside. "Toilets flushing, big sister. Toilets flushing."

Chapter Thirteen

Sunday afternoon, her parents still hadn't called. Anna alternated between fear and relief. Relieved to put off the inevitable confrontation, fear of how upset her parents must be.

When Ryan stopped by, he brought with him a breath of fresh air. And a distraction. In more ways than one.

Her cheeks heated. But that didn't stop her from taking a quick look as he leaned casually against the doorframe.

The blue-gray scarf brought out the sea green in his eyes behind the frames. His denim shirt hung out of his jeans. And his boy-next-door smile made her knees wobble.

Whereas she resembled a big, fat slug. Waiting for a phone call she'd as soon avoid. Like a condemned prisoner waiting to be called out to the firing squad.

He cocked his head. "You're obsessing, aren't you?"

Ryan knew her so well.

She heaved a sigh. "It's not like my dad to hold back." She grimaced. "Which probably means it'll be worse when I finally do hear from them."

He crossed his arms. "Don't borrow trouble."

She gnashed her teeth. "'Cause trouble will find me soon enough."

His lips quirked. "You need something to take your mind off waiting. I have a proposal."

Anna's pulse went into overdrive. Ryan. Her. Making a family for Ruby. Embers of something she hadn't realized she wanted burst into sudden flame.

He grinned. "I know just what we need to do."

What was he saying? Her heart fluttered. Like the wings of a butterfly struggling to be free of a cocoon of its own making.

"I made you a promise. And I aim to keep my word."

A promise? Her head buzzed with a mixture of uncertainty and not-to-be denied longing. What was he about to—

"How about that sleigh ride I promised?"

A sleigh ride. The flutter ceased. The flame extinguished. The embers banked once more, covered with the cinders of hope.

"Feel up to it?"

She faked a smile. "Sure, except it's forty degrees outside."

"You'll need to bundle up. But trust me. I'll take good care of you and Ruby."

Trust him? Ryan was the picture in the dictionary beside *trustworthy*. But it wasn't proving smart to spend so much time with him.

Not smart for her heart. Ryan was leaving. She needed to wean herself from him.

Yet when he stood there grinning at her, she didn't have it in her to refuse him.

She gave a mock sigh. "I guess I can force myself to have fun with you." She wound a scarf around her neck but struggled to button her coat over the bump.

"Let me help." Taking hold of the edges of her coat, Ryan helped her secure the top two buttons.

"I'm afraid button number three is a lost cause."

Ryan lifted her hair out of her collar and fanned it over her shoulders. "There."

His palms lay flat on her shoulders. He stilled. She hardly dared to breathe.

This didn't feel like friendship. What was happening here?

She raised her gaze. His eyes had darkened. But he didn't move. And neither did she. His face with its rugged angles as familiar to her as her own had become unreadable.

Anna ached with a sudden desire to place her palm on the beard stubble lining his handsome jaw. Surely he must be able to hear the beating of her heart. Her eyes locked onto the hollow of his throat, where a vein pulsed.

He lifted her hand to his mouth and brushed his lips against her knuckles. Startled, her eyes flew to his. A tingling shiver that had nothing to do with the cold started at the top of her head and traveled to her boots.

But he dropped her hand. "You're feeling vulnerable." He scrubbed his hand over his hair, leaving it rumpled yet rakishly adorable. "It's those overly emotional pregnancy hormones…"

Was he trying to convince her or himself? She stared at him.

His brows drew together.

That's what it had to be, right? Hormones? She was on pins and needles, dreading the coming confrontation with her parents.

But since returning home, she felt more like herself than she had in a long time. She owed that in large part to Ryan. Perhaps she was imagining this thing between them. Although, after what just happened—

She bit her lip. Nothing had happened. And was annoyed with herself when she couldn't decide if she was happy or sad that nothing had happened.

What would've happened if he hadn't remembered who they were to each other? And who they weren't.

Obviously, she needed a day of fun more than she imagined. "You're not reneging on the sleigh ride, are you?"

"If you're sure you want to go?"

She tromped past him down the steps. "I'm sure."

The sun was high by the time he drove to the farmhouse and hitched Franklin to the sleigh. Woven into the harness, red Christmas ribbons flitted in the wind.

She placed one foot on the bar above the runner. The sleigh rocked. "I feel guilty for taking you away from your responsibilities."

He handed her into the green velvet seat. "You're doing my mother a favor. In the middle of making Christmas candy, words like *underfoot* and *nuisance* were being thrown around before I took off."

She settled into the plush comfort of the upholstery. "I cannot imagine those words describing you."

"Believe it." Climbing into the carriage, he plucked a quilt from behind the seat. "Can't have Ruby or her mother taking a chill." He spread the fabric over her legs.

She snuggled into its warmth. "With Christmas a week away, the garden center must be packed with customers."

"Justine and Ethan have everything under control. Tess is getting the costumes ready for the nativity. Luke's monitoring the tree stand."

"People are still buying trees?"

He sank onto the cushion. "Some families don't put up their tree till Christmas Eve."

"Must be a bunch of 'come heres."

His breath frosted in the wintry air. "It does seem like a waste of a good tree."

"Why not enjoy the lights and decorations as long as possible?"

He gathered the reins in his hands. "Maybe they keep it up till Old Christmas." He smiled. "Maybe you will, too, after this year. Until Ruby's birthday."

She buried her nose in the warmth of her scarf. "But next year you won't be here to see the tree." She sighed. "Or see Ruby."

His smile faded. Ryan clicked his tongue behind his teeth. "Come on, Franklin." The harness bells jingled as Franklin lumbered across the barnyard. "Maybe I will be here when Ruby's born."

She tucked her hands underneath the quilt. "Are you considering staying?" Quick and sudden hope rushed through her.

The sleigh rolled past the farmhouse. "The director of the after-school program resigned. Principal Carden asked me if I'd consider taking the job. If only on a temporary basis until he can fill the position."

Anna's breath hitched. "What did you tell him?"

He loosened his hold on the reins, urging the horse into a gentle trot as they cleared the Christmas tree stand. "I told him I'd think about it." Tugging on the reins, he turned Franklin into the meadow. "What do you think I should do?"

She needed to be very careful what she said. "I'm surprised you'd consider it. You told me how much you've looked forward to getting back to your research. To making a difference."

He leaned forward on the edge of the seat. "After the last few weeks with Oscar, Maria and especially Zander, I've started to wonder, though."

She ran her gaze over the angular line of his jaw. "Wonder what?"

"If maybe I'm making a difference already. Right where I am. How would you feel about me staying in town?"

The wheels of the sleigh clattered over the stones on the trail. Jolting her. Kind of like her heart. Was he talking about staying for a while? Or for good?

She held on to the side. "I think that's up to you to decide what you want. How you want to live your life. Your choice."

Ryan flicked his eyes at her. "I could help you with the baby. Till you get back on your feet."

"Is that the only   ? What good is a few more weeks?"

His jaw tightened. "I thought you'd be pleased I might be able to stay a little longer."

She scowled. "A few more weeks for Zander to get more attached? For Oscar to become more used to having you around?"

For her to become even more attached…

She raised her chin. "If you're going to go, just go."

He closed his fist around the reins. "You sound as if you can't wait to be rid of me."

"It'll be better for Zander—better for everyone—if you make a clean break of it." She gritted her teeth. "Otherwise, they might start imagining you as a permanent part of their lives. They might dream that you're more than just a…" Flushing, she dropped her gaze to the floor of the sleigh.

"We're still talking about the kids, right?" His eyes narrowed. "And you didn't answer my question. How would you feel if I decided to stay?"

"Don't make this about me or the kids, Ryan. Agnes and I will make sure Zander and the rest are okay."

His mouth thinned. "Will you and Ruby be okay if I go?"

Anna pursed her lips. "Stay or go—this needs to be about you."

Somehow, Ryan had turned this on her. What did he want her to say? She'd be devastated when he left.

But if she told him to stay, would one day he resent her for causing him to give up his big chance? Or was he looking for her to absolve him of misplaced guilt?

"You've been a great friend, Ryan. The best. But with Mom and Dad knowing the truth about Ruby…" She struggled to get her feelings in check. "With everything out in the open…"

He looked at her. "Is everything out in the open?"

It was on the tip of her tongue to tell Ryan about the strange yet wonderful emotions he evoked in her heart. But fear held her back.

Fear that he didn't feel the same way. That these last weeks had been about him being a nice guy. About that false sense of responsibility he felt toward everyone. If he decided to stay permanently, the decision had to be about him.

She took a breath. "Mom and Dad will make sure Ruby and I are okay."

His gaze cut to the path. "So you're saying, you and Ruby don't need me anymore."

No, she and Ruby didn't *need* Ryan. As for what Anna wanted? That was another story.

"When do you need to give Mr. Carden your answer?"

A muscle ticked in his cheek. "I told him I'd let him know by Christmas Eve."

She pressed her lips together. "Oh."

Exhaling, he nudged her. "I guess until then you're stuck with me."

She forced a smile. "Stuck."

He cleared his throat. "How about let's go a little faster?" He smiled. "Let's see what ole Franklin can do."

They'd meandered onto one of the farm roads. At her nod, he snapped the reins and urged Franklin into a trot. The winter-bare branches of the forest and the split rail fences whizzed by on both sides of the sleigh. The bells on Franklin's harness jingled in a steady rhythm.

Cold air whistled across her cheeks. With a streak of red, a cardinal alighted onto a branch. She laughed at the sheer exhilaration of the blue sky day and being alive. Ryan grinned, too, the weird tension between them broken.

Reaching the end of the lane, he steered Franklin into a copse of trees. They emerged into the sunlight on the edge of the woods where the embankment sloped into the tidal creek. The scent of pine perfumed the air.

He pulled the reins taut to his chest. "Ho!" Franklin came to a standstill and whinnied.

Looking over the salt marsh, she shaded her eyes with her hand. The water glittered like diamonds. Beyond the uninhabited barrier islands, far on the horizon, lay the sea. Nowhere on the Shore was far from the water.

"It's beautiful."

The reins rested in his lap. "Do you remember how as kids we used to come here in the summer to clam?"

A longing for something she was afraid to name flared within her. "Good times. The best."

He inhaled. "What about if the best is yet to come?"

She gathered her courage. "Maybe it's time for both of us to think more about the future and not the past."

His brows drew together. "Are you truly ready to leave the past behind you, Anna? Are you ready to embrace what could lie in the future?"

Their gazes locked.

"Can you imagine yourself ever loving someone?" He touched her hand. "Or allowing someone to love you?"

The air between them became supercharged.

"If I stayed, could you imagine a future with someone like…me?"

For a second, Anna forgot to breathe. "L-like you?"

His eyes went half-mast. "Like me." He tilted his head and leaned close.

What would it be like to kiss Ryan? Her heart hammered. Was he going to kiss her? Her lips parted and—

His cell rang. Flushing, he pulled away and dug the phone out of his pocket. "What?"

Ethan, he mouthed.

She took the opportunity to replenish her lungs with air. Relief and disappointment. Of the two, disappointment took the upper hand.

He clicked off. "Sorry."

Was he apologizing for almost kissing her?

"Sorry to cut short our ride, but Ethan needs me at the farm."

Perhaps he wasn't apologizing for almost kissing her.

"Another time?" Hoping he understood far more than what she had the courage to say.

He gave her a quizzical look. "If that's what you'd like."

She lifted her chin. "Yes. I would." And next time couldn't come soon enough for her.

Chapter Fourteen

In the school's media center Monday afternoon, Anna put into motion the final surprise the team planned for Maria, Oscar and Zander. To acknowledge their hard work. To celebrate their progress.

Thanks to Mr. Keller's generosity, he was opening his farm to the at-risk students and their families on Wednesday after school for a special Christmas surprise. With Maria's dad holding the reins, the group was going on a hayride. And Ryan's brainchild—Operation Christmas— would culminate with gifts under the tree for everyone.

So in preparation for the occasion, Anna took an inventory regarding Christmas wishes.

"I got my wish." Oscar didn't look up from the holiday picture he was coloring for his new landlady. "There's no rats where we live now, Miz Reyes."

Which nearly sent her into tears. She and Agnes exchanged glances. Swallowing, she made a note to call Brittany.

Agnes, who'd taken charge of coordinating the gift buying, tried another angle. "But if you could get her anything, what would you get for your mom, Oscar?"

"She doesn't need anything." His little face upturned. "My mom's smiling again."

Maria said much the same. "Mr. Keller says I can ride his horses as much as I want." She perked in the chair. "What do you want for Christmas, Mrs. Reyes, more than anything in the world?"

Before Anna could respond, the second grader gave Anna a gap-toothed smile. "I think you should ask for a Christmas baby, Mrs. Reyes, and a handsome teacher man."

Anna's mouth opened and closed.

"The wisdom of children." Agnes chuckled. "Are you smarter than a second grader, Mrs. Reyes?"

She ignored Agnes. "What would your family like for Christmas, Maria?"

Twirling one of her braids, the little girl finally admitted her younger brothers might like a few toys and that her mom could always use a new apron. Or maybe her mom could use a trampoline. On second thought, perhaps a Barbie Dreamhouse.

Anna heaved a sigh. This had seemed easier when she'd thought of the idea.

"I'll do some digging," Agnes promised under her breath.

Returning from a clear-your-head run around the track, Ryan arrived with Zander in tow.

Maria smiled at them. "Are you smarter than a second grader, Mr. Savage?"

"Uh… I guess…" Ryan's brow puckered as Agnes laughed. "Did I miss something here?"

Anna blushed.

Zander flopped into an empty chair. "I'm smarter than a second grader. Because I'm a third grader." And his wish list proved the other extreme from Oscar and Maria. "For Christmas, I want the moon."

Ryan gave him a look. "What else?"

"Stars." Zander shrugged. "And maybe new shoes so I can run away from math."

Ryan rolled his eyes. Anna bit back a smile. She kind of felt that way about math, too.

"How about a new coat instead, Zander?" Agnes waited, her pencil poised over her notepad.

Zander grinned. "Sure. I'm just messing with you, Mrs. Parks."

Later, Ryan pulled Agnes and Anna aside. "Don't worry about Zander's Christmas. I'll take care of everything for his family."

The next few days took on the quality of a surreal dream. A good dream. The kind of dream surfacing from somewhere in the deep places of her heart. An always-there dream. She just hadn't known it. Until now.

Since the sleigh ride, she hadn't been able to spend any time alone with Ryan. There was unfinished business between them. Did he feel it, too?

The piñata proved a huge success with her kindergartners. They took the news about Mrs. Thompson in stride once they learned that Anna would spend the rest of the year with them.

Which reminded Anna she needed to find a caregiver for her baby. She hoped to be able to work until the day of Ruby's birth in January. But afterward, she couldn't afford to take much time off for maternity leave.

As a single parent, her options were limited. Leaving her baby with a stranger wasn't what she'd ever imagined as a girl contemplating motherhood. Agnes, ever connected, would probably have a lead for her to investigate regarding day care.

In addition, there was the looming issue with her parents. Unable to stand the tension any longer, she finally placed a call to them. But no one picked up. She chickened out from leaving a message. After all, what could she say?

As for her personal Christmas wish list? Until returning to Kiptohanock, she would've said she only wanted a healthy baby and a second chance with her family. But now? A handsome schoolteacher featured high on her list.

Her cheeks warmed, recalling Maria's wish for her. She couldn't help but wonder what decision Ryan had made about his future. And if it was a future that included her.

On the last day before winter break, Ryan informed his fifth graders that a new teacher would be taking his place when they returned to school.

There were outcries of dismay. Izzie appeared teary-eyed. Max looked like he wanted to throw something.

"I want everyone to promise me that you'll give the new teacher the respect you've given me."

Matt Evans raised his hand. "You've been the best teacher I ever had, Mr. Savage."

Ryan choked up. "I look forward to hearing great things in the future about what each of you will do to make this world a better place."

There were grudging nods.

He cleared his throat. "I hope you'll return in January with an open heart and mind. Ready to learn." He swallowed. "And make your new teacher as proud of you as I am."

At the end of the day, there were hugs, a quick, fierce one from Max. Ryan turned off the lights and closed the door to his classroom for the last time. How much he'd learned in the last three years. About himself, most of all.

What he'd discovered—he still loved science, but he

loved bringing science alive to kids more. He loved the relationships he'd formed with the children. He loved being a positive role model and influence for good.

He adjusted his glasses. And who would've guessed? He even loved lunch duty.

But about to regain his fondest dream, why were these feelings happening between him and Anna? Perhaps Tessa was right. Was the research job his fondest dream? Maybe his dream had changed.

If he didn't take the directorship of the at-risk program, this would be the last afternoon he'd have with Maria, Oscar and Zander. What a privilege it had been to become part of their lives.

And his heart wrenched at the prospect of parting from them. As for Anna? He tried not to contemplate what it would mean to walk away from her for good.

Brow puckered, she met him outside the front office. "We've got a problem. Zander took the regular bus home."

Ryan frowned. "But why? He knows about the after-school reward."

She crossed her arms over her coat. "Someone told him you weren't coming back to school after Christmas."

"I won't return to fifth grade, but I haven't made a definite decision about the at-risk program yet."

Her eyes glinted. "Well, someone beat you to it."

Ryan raked his hand over his head, dislodging his glasses. "Do Maria and Oscar know?"

"I don't think so."

Ryan heaved a sigh. "How did this happen?"

How had life become so complicated? He should have foreseen this. The elementary school was a microcosm of small-town Kiptohanock.

"I shouldn't have lectured you about coming clean with

your parents when I haven't been able to do the same with the kids."

Her face gentled. "Maybe there's a reason you held back. A good reason."

Ryan shook his head. "I should've been up-front from the beginning. I may have ruined everything with him."

"I told Agnes I'd meet her at Mr. Keller's. The activity bus should be arriving soon. What are you going to do?"

He grimaced. "I'm going to his house to talk to him."

Only when he parked outside Zander's address did he remember the bus driver's warning. About law enforcement and going to this neighborhood alone. It didn't matter, though. He got out of his car.

A man about his age rose from the stoop in front of Zander's unit. "What do you want?"

"My name is Ryan Savage." He extended his hand. "Are you Zander's uncle? I've been hoping to meet you."

"Get lost," the man sneered.

Tensing, Ryan dropped his hand. "Look, I really need to talk to Zander."

Broadening his massive chest, the man clenched his fists. "You don't belong here."

Ryan set his jaw. He had to fix this. He had to make sure Zander was okay. Even if he had to go through Zander's uncle to find the little boy. An uncle with muscled arms the size of small trees at the Savage Farm.

Pushing back his shoulders, Ryan stood his ground. "I'm not leaving until I talk to Zander and make sure he's all right."

"Why do you think the boy is not all right?" the man snarled.

An older lady with tightly wound gray braids shuffled out. "Who you be?" Her dark eyes reminded Ryan of the third grader. Her voice had a Caribbean lilt to it.

"I'm Zander's teacher in the after-school program."

The man jerked his thumb at Ryan. "Are you the one who taught him to make the racket?"

He nodded. "That was me."

"Tapping, Antoine." The old lady planted her hands on her ample hips. "De boy calls it tapping, and it has helped him not be angry. Maybe you should tap, too."

Antoine raised his chin. "So what you do want with him now, Savage? Is he in trouble? What did he do?"

Ryan shook his head. "He's not in trouble. Not at all." He pushed at his glasses. "I'm the one in trouble. He found out something today I should've told him first."

Antoine's eyes beaded. "So you made him cry and—"

"Zander's crying?" Ryan placed his foot on the bottom step. "If I could explain—"

Antoine stepped between him and the door.

"My son be protective of de boy." The older lady made a shooing motion at the man. "Dis be okay, Antoine. I tink Zander should talk to him."

"Just one more man who's let Zander down." Antoine's face resembled carved stone, but he moved aside. "Like me."

She patted Antoine's arm as Ryan moved past. "Dat no' your fault, my son. De Lord say tings be better one day. We hang on and believe."

Antoine snorted. "When has that ever worked for us, Mama?"

The lady ushered Ryan into the small living unit. A kitchen, a bathroom and two bedrooms. Antoine hovered outside.

"Zander." The woman gestured at a closed door. "He upset today."

"I'm so sorry for hurting him, Mrs. Benoit. I never meant…"

"You very important to him." Her eyes drifted to the door. "Dis be hard for Antoine, too. He always important to Zander before…" Her gaze dropped. "Until he get hurt on the job." Her eyes gleamed. "And I be sick."

Ryan should've made a home visit within the first few days of Zander joining his team. Perhaps he or the Parks could have helped the family long before now. "When he missed one of our reward outings, Zander told me that he was helping you."

Her chin lifted. "He be good boy. Antoine had chance to work dat night. And Zander made de choice to miss de milkshake to take care of me."

Ryan smiled. "Zander is a very good boy, and I am proud to know him."

The closed door squeaked. Zander's head appeared in the opening. "Then why are you leaving, Mr. Savage?" His face scrunched, fighting tears. "Did I do something wrong?"

At his grandmother's nod, Ryan went over to the little boy.

"You did nothing wrong, Zan." He crouched to Zander's height. "I'm the one who did something wrong. I should've told you the truth."

Zander's mouth quavered. "Why didn't you, Mr. Savage?"

"I was afraid you'd feel hurt." Ryan touched his arm. "And you got hurt anyway. I'm so sorry, Zander."

Zander crossed his arms over his T-shirt. "Will I ever see you again?"

His heart ached. "I don't know, Zander."

"Are you going to teach a new fifth-grade class?"

"No, I'll be working in a laboratory."

Zander's eyes widened. "With mice?"

"Maybe."

"That's not as cool as teaching, Mr. Savage." Zander launched himself at Ryan, wrapping his arms around Ryan's waist. "You're the best teacher ever. I'm going to miss you, Mr. Savage."

Closing his eyes, he hugged the little boy. "I'll miss you, too, Zan, my man." If leaving was the right thing, why did he feel so torn up inside?

"Don't worry, Mr. Savage. I won't forget about the tapping. And I'll work hard for Mrs. Parks and Mrs. Reyes." He pulled back. "They're not leaving, too, are they?"

"No." He took a breath. "They're staying."

"Good." Zander smiled. "I can't wait to meet the Christmas baby."

But Ryan wouldn't get to meet her.

"Speaking of Christmas?" He consulted his watch. "We still have time to head out to Mr. Keller's if we leave now."

Zander peered at his grandmother. "Can I go?"

Her wrinkled face brightened. "De reward is yours."

"You and his uncle are invited, too, Mrs. Benoit."

Mrs. Benoit cupped her grandson's cheek. "Is dat de truth, Zander?"

"All the families are coming, Gran. Please come. I picked out presents for both of you."

"Go, Mama." Antoine stepped into the apartment. "Enjoy the Christmas food."

"You come, too." Zander moved toward his uncle. "Maria's dad will be there. Oscar doesn't have a dad." He scuffed the floor with his worn-out shoe. "But I got you, Antoine."

Silence hung in the air between them. And Antoine's hard shell cracked. "Yeah, kid." He rubbed his hand across his nephew's short-cropped hair. "You got me."

Antoine followed Ryan in the Benoit family car to Mr. Keller's. The afternoon was chilly, but fun. Due to Mrs.

Benoit's bad knees, she remained in the Keller kitchen to help Mrs. Guzman with meal preparations. The hayride was a blast.

It was with a great deal of pride that Maria, Oscar and Zander presented gifts to family members. And when it was their turn, the front parlor became a hurricane of ribbon and flying paper as the children dove into their gifts.

Mrs. Benoit's cheeks reddened. "I apologize for de mess, Mr. Keller."

"No apologies necessary, dear lady. What would Christmas be without children?" Mr. Keller got misty-eyed. "I can't tell you how long it's been since we had a real Christmas celebration in this old house of mine. I'm the one who should be thanking you for sharing your Christmas with me."

Dinner morphed into an international affair. Mrs. Parks had fixed ham and mashed potatoes. Mrs. Guzman's contribution had a distinctive Southwest flavor. And not to be outdone, Mrs. Benoit added a Creole flair to a dish she whipped up during the hayride.

Even Antoine managed to enjoy himself. Especially when Mrs. Parks put Antoine on the phone with the Reverend about a possible job opportunity at the boat repair shop in Kiptohanock.

His offer to help rejected, Ryan stepped out onto the porch as Mr. Guzman and Mr. Keller took over cleanup duty.

Grabbing her coat off a chair, Anna followed him into the deepening twilight. "I don't know how you did it, but you did a good thing with Zander's family."

He smiled. "Despite the obstacles, I think we can declare Operation Christmas a success." He leaned against the porch railing, taking a moment to enjoy the lavender-pink hues of the sunset.

She rubbed her hands to warm them. "Zander is some kind of proud of that new coat and shoes you bought him." She arched a brow at him. "Wherever did you find the glow-in-the-dark moon?"

Ryan laughed. "He asked for the moon so I got it for him."

"And the stars, too." She smiled. "Every night when he looks at the stars on the ceiling above his bed, he'll think of you."

"Will you?" His heart hammered. "Think of me when I leave?"

"So you decided." She turned her face away, and he could no longer read her expression. "You're leaving."

Why was he fighting this? Why, when a large portion of his heart lay inside Mr. Keller's house right now, shrieking with Christmas delight. As for the rest of his heart? She was standing next to him.

Time to take a risk. There could be no more carefully constructed walls. No more barricades. No more safety net.

Ryan took a cleansing breath of air. "Actually, I'm not leaving."

Her eyes darted to his.

"I've decided to accept Mr. Carden's offer for now. Stay and see where this path leads."

"Where do you want it to lead, Ryan?"

Anywhere with you, he wanted to say. But he didn't. This thing happening between them was as fragile and delicate as a rose unfolding despite the chill of winter.

"Wherever I was always meant to be, I guess. I'm stepping out in faith."

"Placing your dreams in the hands of God." She linked her arm through his. "The safest place your dreams could be." Her lips brushed his cheek.

Inhaling her sweet fragrance, he fingered a silky strand

of her hair. And her eyes—Ryan could get so lost in her eyes—her eyes said to him what her lips could not. Not yet.

Both of them needed time. For Anna to move beyond her first love. For there lay the core of his hesitancy to take a chance on a brand-new future with Anna. Was there room in her life for him?

His dreams might be in God's hands. But his heart… His heart was in hers.

Chapter Fifteen

There was still no word from her parents.

But it wasn't them Anna thought of as she lay awake that night. It was Ryan. Turning over in her mind every look they shared. Pondering the way he made her feel. How *did* Ryan make her feel?

She wasn't sure. He made her feel in a way she'd never imagined to feel again. Ryan was her best friend. Did she want him to be something more?

Taking his shift at the garden center, Ryan called around lunch. "Whatchu doing, Anna Banana?"

Goose bumps pebbled her skin. She wanted to say, *Thinking about you*. But she didn't.

Cradling the phone between her ear and neck, she rested the small of her back against the wall. "I have a late afternoon appointment with the doctor." Her obstetrician had mandated biweekly appointments at this point in the pregnancy. "What have you been doing?"

His voice thickened. "Thinking about you."

And she almost swooned. Who knew Ryan Savage could be so romantic? "I'll see you at the Living Nativity tonight."

"Must I wait so long?"

"Aren't I worth the wait, Mister Sabbage?" she teased.

"You've always been worth the wait, Anna Banana."

She felt breathless. "I'll see you soon." But it didn't feel soon enough.

On the way to her appointment, she stopped by the house. Her firefighter brother, Will, was supposed to come over from the mainland today for the holidays. He and Charlie stood on the porch. She got out of the car and waved at her two younger brothers.

Will enfolded her in a bear-size hug. "Look at you, little mama." He gave her a rakish grin that melted single ladies into a puddle. "How you've grown since I saw you last. Not even a month ago."

"Shut up, you." She swatted at him but allowed him to help her up the steps.

Charlie crossed his arms. "Speaking of mothers? Have you heard from the parents yet, Anna?"

The sinking feeling deepened. She shook her head.

"Me, neither. And I don't like it." Charlie raked his hand over his head. "Leaves me feeling like I'm about to be ambushed."

Will draped his arm around her. "Any other developments to share, big sister?"

"Like what?"

Will smirked. "Like you and Ryan."

Her heart pounded. "I don't know what you mean."

Will and Charlie exchanged glances. "Everyone secretly hoped you and Ryan would get together one day."

She swallowed. "That was then."

Will squeezed her shoulder. "No time like the present."

She frowned. "Ryan and I are friends. He's only staying on a temporary basis."

Charlie shook his head. "I'm thinking it wouldn't take much arm-twisting to change his mind."

She raised her chin. "I don't want him to stay because of me."

Will rolled his eyes. "If not for you, what better reason?"

"I don't need a man to take care of me. I'm a strong, independent woman."

Charlie shuffled his feet on the porch planks. "Maybe too strong and independent for your own good."

She propped her hands on her hips. "How do you figure that?"

"Too stubborn to see what's been right in front of your nose the whole time." Charlie cocked his head. "You may not need him, but how about what you want, Anna?"

What did she want? A real home. And a handsome teacher with beard scruff to love her little, brown-eyed girl.

She blew out a breath. This was crazy. There were other more important issues at the moment. "Can I count on your support when the parents finally do get around to calling?"

Both of her brothers winced, but rallied.

"Of course."

"You know it."

"Thanks, boys." She smiled. "I'll see you tomorrow night at the caroling."

At the doctor's office, she arrived to an overflowing waiting room. Full moon tonight? Was there any truth to the old wives' tale?

The physician's assistant gave her a clean bill of health. "You could deliver anytime."

With the assistance of the lady practitioner, she sat up on the paper-sheeted table. "Not too soon, though. Got to get through Christmas."

The PA made notations on the electronic chart. "Especially with the threat of a winter storm."

She smoothed her skirt. "Snow?"

"Don't we wish. The storm track has the good stuff sweeping north to Pennsylvania."

Anna gave a mock sigh. "Hope for a white Christmas dashed again."

"Better we get nothing than we get ice." The PA patted her arm. "See you next week. Have a wonderful holiday."

"You, too." She inched her way to ground level. Her pulse thrummed with a quiet anticipation at the prospect of seeing Ryan. She arrived at the church to find the rest of the cast already in costume.

Margaret Davenport steered her toward a dressing room. "I was afraid you'd gone into labor."

Catching her eye from across the room, Ryan went into a lopsided grin. Oh, how she liked the way he smiled at her. Her equilibrium went into a nosedive.

Everyone in the Living Nativity took their places outside. Two pint-size shepherds—Izzie Clark and Max Scott—guarded a tiny flock. Their excitement was palpable.

Breaking from the biblical timeline, magi in satin turbans with fake jewels carried gifts for the Christ Child. The foil-wrapped boxes shimmered in the uplighting of the gazebo. One of the kings was Gray Montgomery. And in filmy white layers of angelic splendor, Jade Collier perched on a raised platform beside the makeshift stable.

Anna settled on a wooden stool inside the gazebo. Dressed in his robe, Ryan held a crooked staff. The manger—with a swaddled baby doll—lay between them.

"The scruffy look adds just the right touch."

He pursed his lips. "Why am I not sure if I've been complimented or insulted?"

She adjusted the folds of the muslin shift. A small heater kept the gazebo warm on the chilly night. "It's a compliment. Tessa has you outfitted so authentically you look like you really could be Joseph."

Anna wished Ryan gave himself more credit. He was the kindest, most generous, man she'd ever known. And considering her stalwart band of law enforcement/patriotic male family members, that was saying a lot. But it was true.

The growing line of cars snaked slowly past the square for a gander at one of Kiptohanock's most enduring traditions. Mounted speakers played sacred carols, one after the other.

She imagined bringing Ruby to the Living Nativity next year. Other images raced through her mind. Like walking barefoot on the beach when the weather warmed. Or catching fireflies in mason jars in the summer.

And on the edges of those golden dreams, there was always a handsome teacher. Dare she dream of more for herself and Ruby?

But what about Ryan and his dreams? He'd worked so hard to restart his career. He'd sacrificed so much for his family. Wasn't it his turn now to have his dreams come true?

He rubbed his hand across his beard stubble. "I'm thinking I should probably shave this off before I return to the lab."

"No, don't!"

His eyes widened.

"I mean, I don't think you need to do that." She blushed. "I like you the way you are."

He smiled, a slow upturn of his lips. "Thank you, Anna."

She swallowed. Though quiet, he was a man of great character. Who loved deeply and totally and forever. Could such a love be hers? Is that what she wanted?

The stream of visitors was steady for the next two hours.

She, the demure mother. Ryan, her strong, stalwart champion. Real-life typecasting.

But she couldn't keep her eyes off his face in the glow of the spotlight. Memorizing every line, plane and angle. What was happening to her? She struggled to control her breathing. He would leave Kiptohanock eventually. And she was staying. What possible future could there be for them?

At the end of the evening, the players dispersed. Another successful Living Nativity. Changing into regular attire, she found Ryan waiting, wearing his glasses once again.

"I told Tess I'd lock up."

He walked Anna to her car. Except for the shining star upon the gazebo, the square was bathed in darkness.

Ryan followed the direction of her gaze. "It's on a timer. It'll turn off by itself. No worries."

Easier said than done when it came to life. The insidious fears returned. Should she tell him of her growing feelings? And if Ryan gave up his career goals for her, would someday he come to resent her or worse, resent her child?

If she truly loved Ryan—her dearest friend—she should let him go. To a life that wouldn't include her or Ruby.

"What's wrong?" Always so attuned to every nuance of her feelings, his eyes sharpened. "Are you feeling okay?"

And suppose she convinced him to stay and she lost him anyway? Unshed tears pricked her eyelids. "I—"

"What is it?"

Suddenly, she wanted nothing so much in the world except to feel his lips on hers. She used to daydream in high school that one day he'd kiss her. And tired of waiting, she wrapped her hands around the nape of his neck.

"What are you doing, Anna?"

She tugged his face closer. "Kiss me, Ryan." His mouth was now only inches from hers. "Please. Just kiss me."

His hands, so long-fingered and sturdy, splayed around her upper arms. "Anna…" His chest heaved as if he was having as much trouble breathing as she.

Anna's lips parted.

He kissed one corner of her mouth, but stopped. "Are you sure?"

Anna stood on tiptoe. "I'm sure."

Ryan's blue-green eyes darkened to unfathomable depths. Something seemed to break inside him. The pressure of his fingers around her arms tightened. He covered her lips with his.

Her senses swam. Her knees almost buckled. If he hadn't been holding her up, she might've fallen. But too soon, he stepped back.

"Wow," she murmured, distracted by the spicy male scent of him.

A bemused smile played across his lips. "I'm following you home, Anna, to make sure that clunker of yours gets there safely. See you tomorrow?"

She shook her head, trying to focus. "Tomorrow?"

"The caroling party."

Oh, yeah. That. She nodded.

He held the door for her. "Until then. I can hardly wait."

Neither could she.

Working in the barn on Friday afternoon, Ryan replayed the kiss from last night in his mind. What was Anna thinking? Feeling? Was it possible she wanted a future with him?

He loosened the last of the four bolts, disengaging the wheels from the undercarriage of the sleigh. The forecasters were calling for a light dusting this week.

On the off chance the Eastern Shore actually did manage a white Christmas, he was readying the sleigh for snow. He ran his hand along the length of the sleek runner.

Captivated by the notion of gliding across snowy fields under a moonlit, starry night with Anna in the sleigh. Another opportunity to explore their burgeoning relationship.

Would delaying his departure allow time for Anna's love to awaken for him? His heart turned over in his chest at the lingering memory of their first kiss. Or had love already awakened?

He glanced at the clock. Why wait until the caroling party? Tomorrow was Christmas Eve. He'd go over there right now and surprise her with an early Christmas gift.

Ryan could no longer deny how he felt about Anna. There could be no half-hearted measures involving his feelings for her. Nor in his desire to share a life with her and Ruby. He loved Anna. So much. And Ruby, too.

They, not a laboratory, were everything to him. Why was he holding back? His heart filled with the certainty at the rightness of it all. He didn't want to leave his family. Or Anna and the child they'd raise together. He could make a real difference with children like Maria, Oscar and Zander.

He'd get an early start on showering Anna with what she meant to him. Giving her a small token of the immense gift she was to him. She might not be ready to admit her feelings for him yet. But he'd seen it in her eyes when they kissed.

Ryan loved Anna. Totally. Completely. Forever.

Because he couldn't seem to contain the happiness spilling out of his heart, he borrowed Luke's truck and lowered the wooden cradle into the bed of the Chevy.

At the trailer, with the cradle at his feet, Ryan lifted his hand to knock. The door flew open. And there she stood.

She appeared pleased to see him, a light in her eyes. "I didn't expect to see you so soon."

His stomach muscles tightened. "If you're busy, I'll leave."

"Don't leave." Her hand touched his sleeve as if to hold him there. "Come inside. Please."

"I have something for you." He hefted the cradle in his arms. "Something for the baby actually."

She put her hand over her throat. "You made this for Ruby?"

A sheen of tears welled in her eyes. He set the cradle beside the Christmas tree.

Her finger traced the detail of the woodwork he'd carved into the sides. Thanking him, Anna bobbed in her stocking feet—reindeer socks today.

And he caught her in his arms. Her eyes shining, she kissed him. A kiss as tender as their first. An unspoken promise of more. So much more. A future filled with love and hope.

"Oh, Ryan." Her voice quivered. "How much I—" She pressed her lips together.

Say it, Anna. But she withdrew from his embrace. Leaving his arms feeling empty.

But one day, he promised himself, she wouldn't stop to second-guess her feelings. She'd just love him. Until then…he needed to be patient.

He forced his heartbeat to steady. "I'd better get back. Don't want Luke to dock my pay."

She planted a quick kiss on his cheek.

Dazed, he lifted his hand to touch the spot where the sweetness of her mouth lingered on his skin. "What was that for?"

"One for the road." She hung on the door. "Until tonight."

Chapter Sixteen

Friday night, Anna drove to meet the other carolers. The memory of Ryan's swoon-worthy kiss that afternoon was dancing around in her head. The latest in a growing number of earth-shattering moments. All those years ago, her mother had been correct. A girl had to watch out for strong, silent types like Ryan Savage.

She parked next to the seawall where she could hear the waves lapping against the shoreline below. Her mind flitted to Ryan. Her heart thumped in her chest. Ryan was like still waters and yet somehow altogether more. Like the unrelenting tide of an incoming tsunami.

Anna put her hand on her burning cheek. Her palm felt cold against her skin.

He swept Anna off her feet with the feelings he evoked within her. She couldn't remember the last time she'd been this happy. He unraveled everything she'd believed she'd known and understood and planned. He unraveled her. Ryan would be so easy to love.

If she already didn't. Her breath hitched. Was it true?

Why now? Had the past been only a precursor? So when they came together again, they could more fully appreciate what truly mattered?

Only the stars winked in the indigo twilight above the church steeple. She moved toward the crowd gathered on the church lawn. Her heart lurched as Ryan's gaze locked onto hers.

She slipped through the throng, her greetings on autopilot. In a straight trajectory to the one person who'd made Christmas come alive for her this year. Who'd made her come alive again. His sisters hugged her.

Ryan smiled. "I keep forgetting to ask how the doctor's appointment went?"

Was this possible? Could it be God meant for her to find happiness again? That despite everything, God wanted to give her far more than she'd ever dared to dream?

She gave Ryan a quick medical update as the carolers divided into smaller groups. She and Ryan found themselves with Evy, his sisters and a few Coastie families. Their group would visit the homes around the square.

The carolers fanned out. Some ventured out to outlying areas like the Duer inn or Pauline Crockett's. Another group headed for the hospital. Still another group had shut-ins on their list. Later, the carolers would reconvene at Margaret Davenport's lavish home on the outskirts of town for hot chocolate.

Anna suspected a conspiracy of Savages and Pruitts to ensure she'd have plenty of rest stops. Because on the lawn at each house, an empty chair awaited her.

"You and I are going to take a longer break once we reach your house." His breath warmed her cheek. "And we need to talk." He twined his fingers into hers.

Her heart started to pound. "About?"

Ryan's lips curved. "About us. About the future. I've made another decision."

Her mouth went dry. Was he imagining a future that included her and Ruby? Had he decided to stay for good?

Ryan patted her stomach. "I'm going to have to come up with another fruit name for the little Christmas baby."

"Oh, really?"

"Yes, really, although you don't make it easy." He made a face. "Not much rhymes with Ruby."

She laughed.

He leaned his mouth close to her abdomen. "How does Ruby Red Grapefruit sound to you, little one?"

Movement rippled across the top of her belly. His face transformed with wonder. Ruby most definitely recognized his voice.

"Grapefruit?" Anna laughed. "You are so crazy."

He touched the tip of her nose. "Nippy tonight, isn't it? We better get you inside."

She nodded, her heart full. "Next stop, the Pruitts."

Her arm inserted into the crook of his elbow, they strolled past houses lit with neon Santas, reindeer and the ever-optimistic Frosty. Reaching the family home, Evy's clear soprano started them off with "Joy to the World." Anna sang alto harmony to Ryan's baritone.

Midverse, the door opened, and light spilled onto the carolers. Silhouetted by the interior lights, she recognized her brothers' broad shoulders as they stepped onto the porch.

The carolers had segued to "Away in a Manger" when two other people moved into the doorway. Someone burlier than her brothers. And a shorter, more feminine form beside him. Her throat closed.

Continuing to sing, Ryan glanced at her. She pressed her lips together. *Oh, no. Not now. Not this way.*

But she had only herself to blame. The time for reckoning had come. Her parents stepped into the circle of light. Time had run out for Anna to make things right.

* * *

In the midst of the swelling chorus of voices, Anna let go of his hand. When Evy stopped singing, too, Ryan's gaze shifted to the four people on the porch. And then he understood.

Anna did that protective thing with her hands. One hand on top of her bump, the other cupped the bottom. As if framing her child.

Her father, ex–deputy sheriff Charles Everett Pruitt, Junior, moved to the edge of the top step. The wooden planks creaked. Even in the dim glow of the streetlight, Ryan could tell her father was incensed. Gail Pruitt's eyes were red-rimmed. Their anger and hurt disbelief knifed through Ryan.

"Merry Christmas, Mr. and Mrs. Pruitt," Tessa called.

Evy's coat brushed against him. "Should I get the innocent bystanders away from this train wreck? Or stay here to have your back?"

Justine waved. "Anna didn't tell us you'd be home for Christmas."

Everett Pruitt's face darkened. "Lot of that going around, I hear. The not-telling part."

The chatter faded. An awkward silence reigned. Justine darted an uncertain look at Ryan.

"It might be better, Evy—" Anna sucked in a breath "—if you took the group to the next stop."

Evy bit her lip.

"Please…" Anna whispered.

"Everyone?" Evy's voice took on a crisp, forcibly cheerful librarian tone. "We'd better get going to Margaret's house."

Ryan's sisters didn't budge.

"What's going on, Ryan?"

"What's wrong?"

He nudged his chin to the sidewalk. "It's okay. Go ahead." They left him with reluctance.

"Come inside so we can talk, Anna." Gail Pruitt sounded as if she might burst into tears.

"Mom…" She reached for her mother.

"Go inside the house, Gail." Her father turned the full force of his glare on his daughter.

Fists clenched, Ryan stiffened.

Anna's mother stumbled across the threshold. Will went in after her. Charlie and their father remained.

Ryan helped Anna negotiate the steps. Everett Pruitt took one look at Ryan's hand on his daughter's arm and spun on his heel, disappearing inside.

Charlie waited at the door. "I'm sorry, Anna. They just showed up. No warning."

Moistening her lips, she crossed over the threshold. "The ambush."

"I tried calling your cell, but—"

"But I turned it off when the caroling began." She took a shuddering breath. "This isn't your fault, Charlie." Her voice broke. "It's mine."

Will stepped forward. "And when Mom started to cry…" He hunched his shoulders. "I told them about the IVFs and Mateo's wishes."

Gail Pruitt swallowed. "Why didn't you tell us, Anna?"

Everett shook his head. "Did you think we'd be too stupid to notice you had a baby when we got back from visiting Jaxon?"

"No," she whispered. "I'm the one who's stupid for not telling you before you found out the wrong way."

Everett Pruitt scowled. "Are you telling me that you and Mateo hatched this plot to keep us in the dark over three years ago?"

"It was me. Not Mateo. We believed he would recover,

and we would raise this child together." Her mouth trembled. "It didn't turn out the way we hoped."

"Why now?" Everett rocked on his heels. "Why upend your life after all this time?"

Gail Pruitt's face sagged. "When I think about what you endured alone… Why didn't you tell us, Anna?"

"Because she didn't trust us." Her father's mouth tightened. "She didn't trust her own parents with the second most important decision of her life. Like she didn't trust us enough to tell us before she ran off to get married."

"I was afraid you wouldn't understand." Anna threw out her hands. "Just like you never accepted Mateo."

Everett folded his arms across his barrel chest. "Whose fault was that, Anna?"

Her eyes blazed. "I was afraid you'd try to talk me out of it. Looks like I was right."

Everett jabbed his finger. "You never gave us a chance to know that marine you married. Same song, second verse."

Her breathing had gone shallow. Her face, an unnatural color. She shook like a beech tree in a winter gale.

Ryan took her hand. "This isn't good for Anna. Or the baby."

Everett rounded on him. "You stay out of this. In fact, why don't you hit the road? Stay out of our business, Savage."

Gail Pruitt put her hand to her throat. "We need to talk this through as a family."

Her father glowered at his sons. "Congratulations on the conspiracy of silence. I expected better from you boys."

Will shook his head. "There was no conspiracy, Dad."

"Don't blame them. I asked them to keep quiet until I could tell you myself." She slumped. "Only it took me longer than I'd figured to gather my courage." Her gaze flicked between her parents. "With good reason."

Her father planted his hands on his hips. "Don't you dare blame your mother and me for the choices you've made."

"I don't regret any of my choices. Neither marrying Mateo or carrying his child. They were my choices to make, and I made them."

Ryan winced at the stubborn note in her voice. The situation had taken a turn for the worse. Snowballed out of control.

"In case you're w-wondering, Dad." Her voice quavered. "The baby is a girl."

Her mother's face crumpled. "Why did you shut us out, Anna?"

"I'm sorry for the pain I've caused you, Mom. Dad, I never meant…" Anna choked back a sob.

Everett placed his arm around his wife. "I think we've said everything we need to say. What's done is done." Her father threw a heated glance Ryan's way. "Weren't you leaving?"

Ryan experienced a sudden sympathy for the young, dead marine. He turned toward the door.

"Wait, Ryan." Defiance glinted in Anna's eyes. "I'm leaving, too." She stumbled out the door.

The door closed with a soft click behind them. Raised, angry voices erupted from within the normally tranquil Pruitt home. Closing her eyes, she swayed.

"Let me drive you home, Anna."

"No." She pulled out of his grasp. "I need to be alone." She inhaled sharply. "I want to be alone right now."

Alone? Was he deluding himself about a possible future with Anna? Her father had made an excellent point regarding Anna's past pattern of behavior.

The downside of her fierce independence was a prideful unwillingness to admit she needed help. When she desperately needed it most, she cut herself off from those who loved her most.

Was he fooling himself, imagining something between them? Perhaps he was reading too much into what they'd shared over the last month. Into what she hadn't said.

Doubt ate away at his stomach. His head throbbed. And as he tucked Anna safely into her car, he'd never felt so alone. So cold. Or as empty.

Chapter Seventeen

That night Anna dreamed of Mateo.

Vivid. Painful. Bittersweet. His voice fading, his features becoming less distinct. In the dream, no matter how hard she ran toward him, he remained just out of reach. Until in the end, he was simply gone.

Heart thumping, she jerked awake with a vague sense of loss. She placed her shaking hand atop their child. Proof of what they'd been together.

The essence of Mateo's life went on. The best part of him would always remain with her. She'd never lose him completely.

Ruby lay quiet within her. Untroubled by the grief that beset Anna. She rubbed her hand over her stomach.

The hurt in her mother's eyes and the disappointment in her father's face had been a blow. Distance had yawned between her and Ryan as they walked across the square to her car.

Unable to sleep, she threw aside the covers and swung her feet over the side of the bed. Her legs quivered like jelly. Her ankles were already swollen as if she'd been standing for hours. Or running.

She watched the dawn of Christmas Eve break open

the sky. A flock of blackbirds scratched at the withered brown grass. The anticipated cold front had arrived. Shivering, she warmed her hands around the mug of herbal tea to fight off the chill.

Bundled in extra layers, she checked the thermostat. The trailer felt as cold as it was outside. Like her heart.

She needed to throw off this melancholy. So despite feeling achy, she decided to clean the trailer from top to bottom. The phone rang several times. Each time, she paused in her cleaning frenzy. Listening to the shrill ring of her cell phone. But she didn't answer.

Around lunchtime, she scrolled through the caller ID. The battery needed charging. She'd missed a half dozen calls. From Charlie. From Evy. From Ryan. None from her parents.

Her gut twisted, and she laid down the phone. Her heart hurt almost as much as her aching back. She'd probably overdone it. But idle hands only made for too much introspection.

She tackled the bathroom next. Squatting in the tub, she scoured every crevice. Climbing out carefully, she got on her hands and knees to scrub the peeling linoleum floor. Her loins felt heavy.

Finally taking a break, she pulled a cardboard box out from underneath the bed. Easing onto the floor, she pried open the box containing her life with Mateo. They'd been so in love. So confident of the future. She sifted through the remnants of what used to be her world.

She'd been a student at the university when she met the young marine stationed nearby. At the height of war, rumors abounded that he'd be deployed. Their moments together had been snatched from events out of their control.

Anna squeezed her eyes shut. She hated feeling out of control. Then and now. When Mateo received transfer orders to a base in his home state of Texas, she'd refused to be left behind.

Without consulting her parents, they eloped. Denying her mother a chance to be part of the most important day in her only daughter's life. Shutting them out for fear they'd try to talk her out of what she knew she had to do. No matter the cost.

Only now on the eve of becoming a mother herself did she grasp the betrayal they must've felt. The resentment her parents carried toward the man who in their eyes had taken their daughter from them. Which put Mateo on the defensive. After they married, it had been easier not to come home at all.

It shamed her to realize that the first time Mateo and her parents met had been at Mateo's sickbed. When the cancer had ravaged the body of the once vibrant man she'd married. The grace they'd shown still amazed Anna. Humbled her. And what had she done in return?

Sent them on their way the day after the funeral. So she could put her plans in motion, even as she accepted the folded flag at Mateo's burial. A plan to expunge her guilt for not giving Mateo what he'd wanted most while still alive.

But despite her headstrong willfulness, God had been gracious. Giving her this baby to love. Giving her far more than she deserved.

She closed the cardboard flaps. This box belonged to Ruby. A legacy from the father who would've loved her so much.

Anna rested her head against the mattress. She'd paid a price for loving Mateo when he died. And what about Ryan? Was the price of love too high? Maybe a cost she no longer had the strength to bear.

Overwhelmed, she rested her eyes. But at the sound of

loud caws outside the window, she blinked awake. Disoriented, she glanced at the clock on the bedside table. She must've dozed off.

Muscles stiff, she got on her knees. And using the bed as a support, she towed herself upright. She hung on to the bedpost, slightly nauseous. Ruby hadn't moved since—

Gravel crunched outside the trailer. She twitched aside the curtain as Ryan's Saab parked in the driveway. A dull ache throbbed in her heart. It was nearly dark outside. What should she do about Ryan? What should she say?

But deep inside, she knew what she must do. What she needed to say would hurt him. Yet no matter how much she longed for the safety of his love, she couldn't ask him to stay and deny him his dream.

The path she'd chosen for herself wasn't his to walk. It was a path she must walk alone. After everything he'd sacrificed, she wouldn't hold him back.

It would be so easy to hold on to Ryan. Especially with the turmoil between her and her parents. But her life was a mess, in chaos. And to hold on to him would destroy any chance he had for a new life.

Yet she could never acknowledge to him the real reason she was giving up on them. He'd never put his job ahead of her and Ruby. And so she had to think of another way to make sure he didn't ruin his life. She had to convince him she didn't care for him.

He wouldn't understand. He'd be angry. But she mustn't weaken. She must do what she should've done from the beginning. She rubbed her forehead. The right thing.

Sending Ryan away for good this time. For his good, most of all.

When Anna opened the trailer door, Ryan was filled with a sudden misgiving. He'd spent the previous night battling his own doubts, but determined to trust their relationship. The pallor of her face and the shadows in her eyes sent alarm bells clamoring through him.

He'd called her, but she hadn't picked up. He wasn't worried at first. After the incident with her parents last night, she had a lot to process. Yet as the afternoon dragged into early evening, his willingness to give her space eroded into a gnawing anxiety.

"Why are you here, Ryan?"

He stuffed his hands into his coat pockets. Not the reception he'd been hoping for. Something was wrong. Very wrong.

On shift, Charlie had called Ryan to see if he'd spoken with Anna. Emotions had been high last night. Too high. Anger, betrayal, hurt—a cauldron of swirling bitterness.

"What can I do to help?" He spoke through the open slat of the door. "How can I make things better for you?"

"This has nothing to do with you." Her gaze dropped to her socked feet. Today, snowmen. "This is about me."

Suddenly, everything he held dear was slipping away. Like water running through his fingers, he couldn't hold on to Anna. He was losing her.

And he was desperate. Desperate to take away the expression in her eyes. Desperate for her to once again look at him as she had that night in the gazebo. When he'd believed they might be falling in love with each other.

He placed his foot inside the door. She stepped back, releasing her hold. "Can I come inside? Please, Anna?"

She retreated to stand beside the multicolored lights on the little potted Christmas tree.

His heart thudded. "I know everything looks bleak between you and your parents, Anna. But they love you, and they'll love this baby, too."

Why wouldn't she look at him?

"Just give it time, Anna."

As his hand brushed her arm, her dark espresso eyes lifted. For a fraction of a second, meeting his. With an intensity that stole his breath. And something else. Something that terrified him. Something that spoke of finality.

Her lips parted. He recalled their first kiss. Was it only yesterday? It felt like a lifetime ago.

Ryan stepped forward. Ready to sweep her into his arms. To soothe away the hurts. To love her.

But she didn't move. Instead, her gaze traveled away. Lingering on the cradle he'd made for Ruby.

"I—I..." Anna cleared her throat. "I think I've run out of time."

His stomach knotted. "Anna..."

She shook her head. "I think we've run out of time."

This couldn't be happening. Not after everything they'd shared. Not after the challenges they'd overcome.

"I know you're scared about the future. I'm scared, too. But together..." His voice croaked. "With God all things are possible. We can make a life together. A wonderful life."

He strained forward. Willing her to remember what they meant to each other. He couldn't bear to lose her now.

"Real life doesn't work that way, Ryan."

"God brought us together again, Anna." He clenched his hands at his sides to hide their trembling. "We're meant to be together."

A vein pulsed in the hollow of her beautiful neck. "I can't do it. I can't open myself up to someone again. I can't face the hurt."

"I'd never hurt you, Anna." He swallowed. "I love you."

She closed her eyes. "Don't say that."

"Look at me, Anna." His tone roughened. "You love me, too. I know you do."

She opened her eyes. "Love is a choice. A choice I made once before. A choice I refuse to make again. Hurt—no matter how much you deny it—is inevitable."

He had to do something. Stay calm and make her see… "I'm not going to die like Mateo."

Anna laughed, a short, clipped sound. "Mateo didn't believe he'd die, either. But he did."

"So you're going to cocoon your heart forever on the off chance someone is going to leave you?" Despite his determination to remain calm, anger laced his words.

"I'm not strong enough to survive another loss, Ryan."

"What kind of life is that, Anna?" He scrubbed his hand over his face, dislodging his glasses. "What kind of life is that for Ruby?"

She framed her belly with her hands. Shutting him out. Protecting Ruby from him. "I should've never—"

"You *love* me." He straightened his glasses. "This is about you being scared of losing control." He didn't know what to do with his hands. "Love is a choice to trust each other more than you need to be in control."

She lifted her chin. "I can only trust in my love for my baby. There's no room for anyone else."

His eyes burned. "Love doesn't have to work that way, Anna."

"This was a mistake, Ryan. *We* are a mistake."

He reeled as if she'd slapped him.

She squared her shoulders. "I can never repay you for what you've done for me."

"You don't owe me." Her words sparked a fuse inside him. "I did everything because I love you. Because I want us to be a family."

"We can never be a family, Ryan. I can never love you the way you want because…" She took a deep breath. "Because I will never stop loving Mateo."

He staggered. What he'd feared from the beginning. Flaying open the root of his insecurity. The resignation in her eyes drained the last of his resistance. A living man he could fight. The memory of a dead hero he could not.

"You should go." Anna moved past him. "There's really nothing to keep you in Kiptohanock past Christmas. You should take the job in North Carolina."

This couldn't be how it ended between them. This was like a nightmare from which he couldn't awake.

"I probably won't see you again before you leave. This is for the best. A clean break. A fresh start." She gulped. "For both of us."

She didn't love him. She didn't want him in her life or Ruby's. This wasn't the Christmas he'd envisioned. This wasn't the future he'd hoped to share with Anna.

He was so stupid. Blinded by his feelings for her. This is what came from letting down his walls. Had he learned nothing after what happened with Karen? He'd been about to give up, yet again, the life he'd worked so hard to return to.

Thank God, he hadn't yet called Mr. Carden or his boss in North Carolina.

By blurting out how much she'd come to mean to him, he'd lost her friendship, as well. And the chance to be a part of Ruby's life. A hollow pit opened in his heart.

He extended his hand. "Can I say goodbye to Ruby?"

Anna's eyes glittered, but she nodded.

His fingertips brushed the fabric of the red wool sweater. Beneath his touch, Anna quivered.

"Goodbye, little one." His vision blurred.

"Ryan…" Anna laid her hand over his for an instant. "I'm so sorry."

Flinching, he pulled away. "Goodbye, Anna."

And stumbled out the door as night descended. Falling

like a cloak over the sky. A deep darkness as heavy as his heart. As bleak as the life he was destined to live alone.
Without Anna. Without Ruby. Without love.

Chapter Eighteen

The red taillights of Ryan's car disappeared into the night. Anna hadn't expected the pain lashing her heart to hurt so deeply. As if a part of her had died—as if an essential organ had been taken from her.

Phantom pain? Veterans missing limbs spoke of the strange ache—a throbbing pain where none should exist. And she wondered if the heart worked that way, too.

Her heart had broken at the stunned look on his face. At the pain she caused him. But she couldn't turn back now.

She'd done the right thing in setting him free. He deserved better than someone's widow. More than someone else's child. Yet she could hardly bear the wrenching despair in his eyes when she sent him out of her life for good.

A snowflake drifted from the sky. The snowflake became two. Then, as if an atmospheric switch had been flipped, more flurries than she could count.

Just in time for Christmas. But she felt only a hollow emptiness. Had Ryan been by her side, they would've run outside together to revel in the glorious display of winter's splendor.

He was the one person with whom she could share anything and everything. The pain in her back fisted. Ryan's friendship was the true constancy in her life.

Ryan loved her. She rubbed at the throbbing ache in her lower back. She couldn't think of that now, of a future never meant to be.

The pain intensified. Had her emotional pain prevented her from appreciating the beautiful gift of Ryan's love? A gift from God. Had she done the right thing in sending him away?

Cold air leaked through the glass pane. Wind gusts sent the flakes whirling. The snowfall had become a torrent of swirling white.

Her pulse ratcheted. Snow blanketed the grass, obscuring the driveway. But she was safely cocooned from the storm. Although... She examined the thermostat.

The interior temperature had dropped. How was that possible? She pressed the button to raise the temperature. But the number on the dial didn't change. Frowning, she pressed harder. Nothing happened. She thumped the box on the wall.

With mounting concern, she headed toward the floor register near the sofa. Wincing, she got on her knees. She placed her hand over the vent, expecting a rush of air on her skin. Nothing.

Painfully, she heaved herself to a standing position. She'd put on more layers. And wait out the storm. Come morning, everything would be fine.

She'd taken two steps when a rush of oozing liquid seeped through her leggings. Anna stared at the puddle between her feet. Her water had broken. The lights on the tree blinked out, and the trailer went dark.

Ryan intended to go home. But he found himself driving toward town. Like most of Kiptohanock, his family would already be at the candlelight service.

Part of him wanted nothing more than to be alone. To find a place where he could give full vent to the anguish consuming him. But his wounded heart needed something else. He needed to wrap himself in the loving embrace of his heavenly Father.

He steered past the Coast Guard station, where he spotted Chief Scott's truck. It was like Braeden Scott to pull Christmas Eve duty so others under his command could be with their families. Dark clouds scrolled across the watery horizon. He hoped the squall stayed out to sea.

If the storm took a more westerly course, emergency responders were in for a difficult night. Ice storms could knock out power, take down trees and result in multiple vehicular incidents.

He parked in the church parking lot as the first snowflake fell. Light glowed from inside the building. Organ music poured outside the walls of the white clapboard church.

Silent night, holy night. All is calm. All is bright.

Getting out of the car, he lifted his face. The floating snowflakes settled cold upon his cheeks. At last, a white Christmas.

Ryan yearned for God's comforting peace. He felt so alone, so bereft. The encroaching storm winked out what remained of the stars overhead.

He inhaled, the cold stabbing his lungs. "Show me what to do, God. Show me how to live without Anna."

Cries of childish delight erupted around him. Despite his heartache, he smiled at the antics of the children spilling out of the sanctuary. Tongues protruding, Max and Izzie strained to catch their first taste of snow. Others followed. Young and old. Arms extended to embrace the joy of snow, their faces exhilarated.

Laughing and shivering, Reverend Parks called his

church family inside. Out of the dark. To rejoice together on this most glorious of nights.

Ryan tromped in with the rest. From the deep casement windows, thick white candles in hurricane lanterns flickered within the sanctuary. There was an air of luminous expectancy. He found solace in the words of the music flowing around him. Comfort in the company of family and friends.

O little town of Bethlehem, how still we see thee lie...

Seth's gravelly bass boomed from the Duer row. Amelia and her brood. Caroline, her husband and Izzie. Sawyer with one arm draped around Honey, who held baby Daisy on her hip. His other arm around his long-lost sister, Evy. Love lost, love recovered.

Above thy deep and dreamless sleep, the silent stars go by...

The Colliers stood behind the Duers. Their son, Gray. With his rusty baritone, Canyon sang between Kristina and Jade. And bound by ties of love and friendship, Margaret Davenport.

As Ryan eased into the family pew, his mother's forehead puckered. Somehow without being told, she always knew when one of her children hurt. He felt Tessa and Justine's searching scrutiny. The music and the voices flowed around him. *Yet in thy dark streets shineth, the everlasting light...*

Across the aisle, Everett Pruitt appeared the picture of despondency. Gail Pruitt's shoulders slumped. An empty space remained for Anna. But she wasn't coming.

He met her brother's dark eyes. He shook his head at Will's unspoken query. *The hopes and fears of all the years are met in thee tonight.*

Reverend Parks lit the first votive. Ryan fumbled in the

pew rack for the small candle, encircled by a ring of cardboard to prevent hot waxy drips.

Seth and Everett stepped forward. Reverend Parks touched his flame to their wicks. Everett began with his own family. His wife lit Will's. On the other side of the aisle, Seth lit Evy's votive first. She passed the gift of light to Sawyer and so forth down the line.

In harmonious synchronization, the two elders worked their way from row to row. Pauline Crockett. Mr. Keller. The Evans family. Coastie families stationed in Kiptohanock. Dixie and Bernard. Ryan and his mother. Justine. Tessa. Ethan and Luke.

Until the final candle was lit, and everyone's features shone in the glow of the candlelight. The darkness pushed back. Hope reborn.

A holy hush fell over the sanctuary. Reverend Parks read the Scripture passage from Luke chapter 2. Peace soaked deep into the core of Ryan's being.

Beyond his own heartache, he ached for Anna's self-imposed isolation. The immensity of the journey she was determined to undertake alone.

As an unsettling disquiet descended on Ryan, the outer doors of the church banged open. One of the children cried out. Everyone jolted as the fury of the wind whistled into the church.

In the fierce onslaught of the wind, Chief Braeden Scott struggled inside. "The storm took an unexpected detour. Forecasters are predicting heavy snow followed by dangerous ice."

Reverend Parks took charge. "Driving will become hazardous. Everyone needs to get home as quickly as possible."

The piercing wail of the fire siren punched through the roar of the wind. Evy looked up from her phone. "Charlie says Highway 13 is impassable in places. There are already lots of traffic accidents."

Will stepped into the aisle. "I'm going to head across the square. Any trained volunteers will probably be helpful tonight."

EMT-trained Luke shouldered his way past the others to follow Will into the snowstorm.

The congregants scattered. Chief Scott hugged his wife and returned to the station. Ryan and Ethan hustled the family outside. He gasped at the transformation. The night had become a hurricane of white. Snow blanketed the streets.

His mother grabbed his arm. "Leave your car. Ride home with us."

But urgency frayed at the hard-won peace he'd attained inside the church. Across the square, the town's lone ambulance became mired in a snowdrift. He exchanged a long look with Ethan, who possessed a rudimentary knowledge of first aid thanks to Uncle Sam.

Ethan tossed Ryan the car keys. "Make sure Mom and the girls get home."

"I'll leave my car for you and Luke." Ryan touched his brother's shoulder. "Be careful out there tonight. You're not as indestructible as you'd like us to believe."

His brother's eyes clouded as they often did since returning home from his deployment. Ryan wasn't the only walking wounded in the Savage clan.

Ethan nodded. "It's going to be a long night." Then he hastened through the snowstorm.

Parked next to the Scotts, Ryan helped Seth secure little Patrick into his car seat. Max scraped the windshield as Amelia cranked the engine to warm the vehicle.

His mother scrambled inside the Savage family's SUV.

His sisters got to work on the windshield. "We got this, Ryan," Justine called.

"Papa Seth?" Patrick's brow furrowed. "How's Father 'hanock gonna find us in the storm?"

"Don't you worry none 'bout him." Seth clicked the final strap in place. "Every good father always finds those who belong to him."

The girls ducked inside the SUV as Ryan wrenched open the driver side door. *Every good father...* He'd never have the privilege of being Ruby Reyes's father. He started the car.

He glanced in his rearview mirror at the open bay of the fire station. With Luke behind the wheel, the other volunteers attempted to rock the immobilized emergency vehicle into forward motion.

Leaving town, it was all Ryan could do to keep the SUV from blowing off the road. With the yellow lines no longer visible, he relied on instinct and memory as they inched slowly homeward. Whiteout conditions prevailed. The windshield wipers hardly made a dent against the driving snow. He was thankful Anna hadn't ventured out to the service.

On the snow covered bridge spanning a tidal creek, the rear tires slipped. Tessa gasped from the back seat. He steered into the slide and fought the instinct to jerk the wheel. In the passenger seat, Justine grabbed hold of the dashboard.

Somehow the tires found traction. The car lurched forward onto solid ground. But bowed by heavy snow, tree branches snapped on both sides of the road, the sound like shotgun blasts. A thud shook the ground.

Tessa swiveled. "A tree's fallen across the bridge. That could've been us."

"Which means no one can get in or out of Kiptohanock

until a crew clears the road." His mother bit her lip. "We need to pray we make it home."

He already was.

Anna didn't panic—not too much anyway—when the lights went out. She'd probably been in labor at least twelve hours. She needed to deliver within twenty-four hours or risk infection. And the clock was ticking.

Despite the unusual circumstances of Ruby's conception, hers wasn't a high-risk pregnancy. At thirty-eight weeks, Ruby was well within the accepted timeframe for a healthy delivery. But Anna needed to get to the hospital and soon.

A contraction took her breath. She bent double, sweat breaking out on her forehead. If she hadn't been so stubborn…she'd be with Ryan and her family at the candlelight service.

Only one bar glowed on her cell phone, eerily green in the darkness of the trailer. She'd forgotten to recharge it. Pain buckled her knees.

Gasping, she sank onto the mattress, the phone gripped in her clammy hand. She called 911, but no one picked up. She clicked off and tried again. Still no answer. Dispatch must be logjammed.

Praying she had enough power for one more call, she called her dad. No matter how angry or disappointed, her father had never let her down.

As the phone rang, she visualized the comforting warmth of her childhood home. The sturdy Victorian filled with light. The flames in the hearth. Her mother's ham roasting in the oven. The images were so tangible, she pressed her lips together to keep from crying aloud.

"Please pick up… Where are— Hello? Dad, is that

you?" But it was only voice mail. "I'm going to drive to the hospital, Dad. If you get this message, meet me—"

The phone blanked out. And with it, the last of the power drained away. She stared at the dead phone in her hand, unable—unwilling—to face the enormity of her aloneness.

No one was coming to rescue her.

She'd pushed everyone away. She'd demanded to be left alone. She was as alone as she'd ever been in her life. Stranded and in labor.

Pushing off the bed, she pulled on her red peacoat. She set her jaw. She'd do this like she'd done everything else. The fertility treatments. The multiple IVFs.

Buttoning her overcoat wasn't an option, but she donned a knitted wool cap and gloves. She also wrapped a heavy wool muffler around her neck. Suitcase in hand, she opened the door and stepped into a maelstrom of ice pellets. The wind snatched the door from her grasp and banged against the interior wall.

Setting the suitcase on the steps, she wrested the door closed. The steps were slick and treacherous. The wind buffeted her as she clung to the railing Ryan had installed. Ice shards stung her eyes and cheeks. She buried her face inside the scarf.

The ground crunched beneath her boots. Not a good sign. Too many small bridges spanned the tidal marshes between her reaching help. And bridges iced first.

Her heart beating like a drum, she tensed as another contraction seized her midsection. Squeezing. Crushing. Robbing her of coherent thought until the pain subsided.

Jamming the key into the ignition, she cranked the engine. But the motor only coughed.

"This cannot be happening." She turned the key again. "Please, please…"

She held her breath. The engine sputtered but caught. Shifting into gear, she inched down the driveway. The wipers beat a losing fight to keep pace with the whirl-wind of sleet.

"Come on…come on…" she coaxed the Volkswagen. "Don't give up on me now. We've come too far together, old friend."

The front tires spun. She pressed the accelerator to the floor and gunned the engine. The car surged onto the main road. But the headlights provided only the smallest amount of visibility.

Pain began low in her loins and spread upward. Steal-ing her breath. Making her legs wobbly. Her senses swam.

Was it her imagination? Or had the force of the wind abated somewhat? The Volkswagen no longer rocked. She crept forward, pushing the odometer as fast as she dared.

Ice stopped pelting the windshield. She took courage as the vehicle passed over the first bridge. She strained forward against the steering wheel as if by sheer force of will, she could speed the little car on its way.

As she approached the next bridge, how she wished Ryan was with her. She was so tired of battling alone.

Why had she said those horrible, untrue things to him? She loved him. Part of her had always loved him, as a best friend. Until without realizing it, her feelings for him had grown into so much more.

Anna wanted to feel his arms around her again. As soon as Ruby was born, she'd find Ryan and beg for his for-giveness. She'd plead for him to give her another chance. She just wanted to be wherever Ryan would be happy— North Carolina or home in Kiptohanock. Whichever made him happy.

She started to exhale as the front tires safely exited the slippery surface of the bridge. Then, the rear end of the car fishtailed. Instinctively, she removed her foot from the accelerator and fought to control the wheel. But it was already too late.

Ryan breathed a sigh of relief as he rounded the bend toward the farmhouse at the end of the lane.

Every good father... His father had been the best. Ryan's hero.

His mother and sisters struggled into the house. He headed to the barn to check on the backup generator. The familiar, comforting scent of hay, horse and leather tickled his nostrils.

But his heart remained troubled. Something wasn't right. He didn't know what exactly. The phone in his pocket buzzed. Stamping his boots free of snow, he took out his phone and glanced at the display. Pruitt, E.

Why would Everett Pruitt call him? He wasn't exactly on Pruitt's list of favorite people.

Every good father... He frowned. He wasn't anybody's father. Nor likely ever to be.

"What?" he growled into the phone.

A beat of silence.

"Is that you, Ryan?" Everett Pruitt cleared his gruff voice. "I'm sorry to bother you on a night like this...but it's Anna."

Sudden fear seized his heart. "What about Anna?"

"I turned on my cell when I got home, and there was a message from her. She's in labor and driving to the hospital. The call dropped. I dialed her number, but I couldn't get a signal."

Ryan's heart thudded. "She shouldn't drive. The roads are terrible." He scrubbed his forehead. "And the bridge out of town is impassable. The ambulance can't come to her. What about 911?"

"Dispatch has been overwhelmed with folks caught in the snow squall." Everett sighed. "I messaged Charlie to go the long way around from the other side. But there's a tangle of accidents clogging the highway. Fallen trees and power lines are lying everywhere. It's going to take him a while to get there."

If even then… And Anna was out there, isolated and alone.

"This is my fault." The unflappable former lawman's voice broke.

Ryan clutched the phone. "I shouldn't have left her this afternoon. No matter what she said."

"If anything happens to my girl, I'll never forgive myself." Everett took a ragged breath. "I'm not used to doing nothing. I don't know how to help her."

Ryan's throat constricted. She must be so frightened. What would happen to Ruby? Would anyone be able to get there before it was too late?

Tessa's horse, Franklin, pawed the stall. And Ryan had an idea. A desperate, last-ditch idea.

"Mr. Pruitt? I might know a way." He gripped the phone in his hand. The best way—perhaps the only way—to reach Anna.

Every good father…

"I'm taking the sleigh to look for her." He pressed the cell to his ear. "Have the Kiptohanock EMTs waiting for us. But no matter what, I promise I'll bring Anna home to you, Mr. Pruitt."

As Ryan ended the call, he prayed as he never had before.

Chapter Nineteen

The VW careened toward the bridge railing. Anna clawed at the wheel. With a sickening jolt, metal impacted metal. She screamed.

Ricocheting, the car plummeted down the embankment. In a cacophony of horrific screeching noises, the Volkswagen skidded toward the black water before settling with a final crashing shudder.

Landing engine-first in the creek, the rear end stuck straight out of the water. Moaning, she clutched her abdomen. Was the baby okay?

Something freezing cold seeped into the soles of her boots, and she stared in disbelief as marsh water rose from the floorboards. Frantic, she plucked at the seat belt. If she didn't get free—

The lock released, and with a fear born of adrenaline, she scrambled—belly and all—between the front seats.

In the back seat, she wrenched at the door handle. Nothing. But bracing her boots against the door, she shoved. Trapped against the snowpacked embankment, the door yielded a foot. Not much, but enough.

By holding her breath and sucking in her gut, she squeezed through the narrow opening. Like a cork out of a bottle, she popped out. Only to find herself losing the battle with gravity.

Sliding on the ice-coated bank, she flailed, reaching for anything to stop her descent. She fell against the car.

Tears matted her eyelashes and froze. She groaned as another contraction knifed through her. An excruciating minute before the worst of it passed. No one knew where she was. And with the car sinking into the marsh, no one would think to look for her down here.

She fought her way inch by painful inch to the top of the embankment. For Ruby's sake, she couldn't quit.

Using the dented railing on the road for support, she staggered to her feet. The snow had stopped, but drifts blanketed both sides of the road. It was hard to tell where the pavement ended. She didn't want to end up in the creek again.

Shivering, she pushed onward, one step after the other. If she stopped, she'd die. And so would Ruby.

But her foot came down on nothing, and she stumbled. Falling, she twisted to avoid crushing the baby. Landing on her back, the breath whooshed out of her lungs.

She lay there, stunned. Cold and tired. Tired of fighting to remain alive. She closed her eyes. She needed to sleep. Just a few minutes.

From beneath her closed eyelids came the image of Ryan's face when he kissed her. Followed by another picture of Ryan holding her baby, loving her baby. Loving Anna. A scene with no basis in reality. Not yet…

Her eyes flew open. Her heart hammered. She had to get out of here. With a biting snap, her numbed limbs tingled painfully to life.

But she'd reached the end of her delusions of self-sufficiency. "God, help me, please." Her voice rang out over the hushed stillness.

And that was when she heard it.

Bells. The jangle of a harness. The sleigh? Had Ryan come looking for her?

Rolling onto her side, she planted her mittens into the snow and pushed upward. She had to get his attention. It was now or never. "Ryan!"

The wind caught her voice and snatched it away. Panic swelled. He'd pass by without seeing her.

The sleigh glided along the ice-encrusted roadway. Franklin's breath puffed in the cold, night air. But at the edge of the wood, movement caught Ryan's attention. Contrasted against the snowy landscape, something red.

His lungs burned as he sucked in a blast of frigid air. Yanking the reins, he jerked Franklin to a standstill. "Anna?"

God, please let it be Anna. Where was her car? What was she doing out here on foot?

Tossing the reins onto the seat, he plunged out of the sleigh, only to flounder in the knee-deep drift. Grabbing hold of the bridle, he led the horse down the gentle slope to the other side.

"Anna!"

She raised her head. "Ryan... I—"

Dropping the bridle, he ran to her side. "I'm here, Anna. It's going to be okay." Gathering her in his arms, he lifted her off her feet. He slogged toward the sleigh. "You need to get warm."

She tucked her head underneath his chin against the hollow of his throat. "I'm so sorry, Ryan. For everything."

He set her on the seat, but she clung to him. "Don't leave me, Ryan. Please..."

Ryan's heart thumped. "Let me get the quilt." He eased out of her stranglehold. "I'm not going anywhere. I'll be here as long as you need me." He wrapped her in the quilt. "But I'm going to have to help Franklin find the way home."

She huddled into him.

Cutting a path through the forest, he kept the sleigh off the road. There was one place where they could bypass the fallen tree blocking the entrance to town. He'd have to risk fording the tidal creek near a shallow, narrow portion of the marsh.

"We're almost there, Anna." He drove Franklin as hard as he dared. "Hang on."

She bit off a groan. His eyes darted to her. Contorted with pain, her face was pale.

"Do I need to stop?"

She gritted her chattering teeth. "K-keep g-going." Her breathing became labored as she fought the next wave of surging pain.

Franklin came to an abrupt halt at the incline leading into the creek. Jumping out of the sleigh, Ryan's boots thumped on the snowpacked ground. He grabbed Franklin's bridle. The horse tossed his head, but Ryan hauled the horse forward.

Never letting go of the bridle, he guided Franklin into the water. The sleigh jolted over the pebbled creek bottom. Anna clutched the side of the sleigh as the horse clambered up the creek bank. And they emerged beyond the blocked bridge.

The whirring red and white lights of the waiting ambulance were a welcome relief. Luke got out of the driver side. Her father clambered out the passenger seat. The back doors of the ambulance swung open to reveal Will and Anna's mother.

Ryan swallowed. He'd not realized how scared he'd been

that he'd have to deliver the baby by himself. "Look who's here to meet their grandchild, Anna."

Her parents hurried toward the sleigh.

"Mom? Dad?" Tears clogged Anna's voice. "I'm so sorry. For everything."

Will and Luke followed with a gurney.

"Daddy…" She sobbed as Ryan lifted her out of the sleigh. "If you and Mom could ever find it in your heart to forgive me…"

Everett Pruitt's stern features softened. "All's forgiven, honey." He reached for his daughter. "Thank you, Ryan, for everything you've done. I'll take it from here."

Ryan hesitated only an instant before he surrendered Anna into her father's arms. Everett laid her on the gurney.

Her mother went into nurse mode, checking Anna's vitals. "She'll never make it Riverside, not with the road conditions. Take her to our house." She exchanged glances with Will. "We're going to have to deliver this baby ourselves."

Will's dark eyes—so like Anna's—clouded. Luke took Mrs. Pruitt's place beside the cart. Silent, Ryan stood beside the panting horse as the men rolled the gurney into the ambulance.

Anna stretched out her hand. "Where's Ryan?"

Everett's eyes shot to him. "He's not far, sweetheart. He'll follow us to the house, right?"

Ryan gave a quick jerk of his head. He'd planned on coming, invitation or not.

Everett stroked the hair off her perspiring forehead. "Ryan will see you soon. Just hang in there."

The wheels folded as they lifted the gurney into the ambulance. Her mother jumped in with Will. Everett jogged around to the passenger side.

Luke slammed the doors closed. "Take the horse to the

firehouse, Ryan. Ethan will take care of him. And get out of those wet boots."

The ambulance disappeared around the square toward the Pruitt home. Anna had asked for him. And for now, that was enough.

Leaving Ethan to deal with the horse and sleigh, Ryan tromped through the snow on the square. Except for the chugging whine of an outdoor generator, the streets lay dark and quiet. When the transformer blew, Kiptohanock's electricity went with it.

It was late. Most folks were probably waiting for the dawn under thick, heavy quilts. Tomorrow was Christmas morning. He could only imagine Anna's weariness. It had been a long, excruciating evening. And it wasn't over yet.

But at the end of weariness lay joy. By tomorrow—God willing—she'd be a mother. The Pruitts would have a new baby to love.

As for him? When the highway cleared, would he find himself driving away to the start of a new life? At the Pruitt house, he climbed the creaking steps to the wrap-around porch.

Stomping the snow from his borrowed boots, he was about to knock when Evy threw open the door. "Thank God you're here." She yanked him inside.

At the base of the staircase, Everett wrenched Ryan's coat off his back. "Anna's calling for you. We can't get her to settle. You'll need to stay with her."

"Uh…" His gaze ping-ponged around the parlor, where logs blazed in the hearth. "During the delivery?"

He'd imagined the scenario in so many different ways. Pacing a hospital corridor and waiting for news. Or in his new condo in North Carolina, getting a phone call from

Anna. But never this. Being an active participant in the most wondrous moment of her life.

Flashlight in hand, Will appeared on the landing. "Anna wants you, Ryan."

If only that were true. He scrubbed his chin with his hand. But it wasn't true. She needed her friend. Nothing more. She'd come to depend on him over the last month of her pregnancy.

Yet despite the unfulfilled longings of his heart for Anna, he was grateful for the opportunity to see the little Christmas baby born into the world.

He followed Will upstairs to the room that had always been Anna's. The glow of candles pushed the darkness to the corners. Propped in the bed, she gripped her mother's hand. Her chest heaved.

As his shadow fell across them, Mrs. Pruitt glanced up. "I wasn't sure how much longer she could hold out." She beckoned him to take her place beside the bed. "Anna, sweetheart? Ryan's here. I need to check your progress. I think it's about time to push."

Sinking onto the footstool, he grasped Anna's hand. Sweat glistened on her forehead. Her eyes were large with fear and pain. "Ryan…"

"You're going to get through this," he whispered. "You're strong and brave and beautiful."

There were times when she squeezed his hand so hard he lost feeling in his fingers. Her mother and Evy stationed themselves at the end of the bed, beyond the tented sheet lying across her knees.

Lines creased her forehead. Her chin sank onto her chest as her body hunched. But her eyes never left his face.

"Breathe, Anna," he encouraged. "You're doing great. Just a little more."

One final, agonizing push. Mrs. Pruitt opened her

hands. Anna fell onto the pillows. Tears streamed across Evy's face. Will grabbed a pair of scissors.

"Mom," Anna gasped. "Is my baby all right?"

There was a high-pitched cry of tiny outrage.

"She's perfect." Gail Pruitt's face shone. "Absolutely perfect."

Anna struggled to sit upright. "I want to see her."

Evy spread a towel on the bed. Mrs. Pruitt laid the writhing pink bundle on top and wrapped the baby in its warmth. She placed the baby alongside her mother.

A tiny fist waved in the air. And a small foot shot out from beneath the folds of the towel. Anna's eyes darted to his.

She laughed. "No surprise there, huh?"

He swallowed past the lump in his throat. "A girl who's got something to say. And she intends to say it."

Ryan fell to his knees beside the bed as Anna cradled her long-awaited child. Her Christmas baby.

Anna brushed her lips against her daughter's delicate cheek. "Hello, Ruby Gail Reyes."

Her mom's mouth trembled.

Lured by the lusty cries of life, her dad ventured into the room. He draped his arm around his wife. Gail Pruitt leaned her head on his shoulder.

"I'm naming her for Mateo's grandmother and my amazing mom." Anna moistened her lips with her tongue. "I pray I can be as incredible a mother as she has been to me."

The tough ex-deputy didn't look so fierce now. His eyes were red-rimmed. Ruby Gail Reyes had reduced the blustering lawman to emotional gelatin.

Will cleared his throat. "She's like a baby football."

Anna rolled her eyes. "Only a Pruitt would think that."

"We should clean her up," Mrs. Pruitt added.

"Just a few more minutes." With Ruby tucked in the crook of her arm, Anna unfolded the towel. "After I count her fingers and toes." She looked at Ryan. "Wanna help? Since I know math is kind of your thing."

And so together they counted each one. While Ruby Reyes let the world know how she really felt.

He rose. "All present and accounted for."

Anna gazed at him, her arms outstretched. "Would you like to hold her, Ryan?"

His heart jackhammered. "Yes." He gulped. "I would."

For a second, the baby lay in both their arms as she transferred her hold to him. A moment in which he had eyes only for Ruby's mother. The great love of his life.

The only love of his life. And he beheld in that fraction of a heartbeat the life that could never be his. The love that would never be his. A woman whose heart would always belong to her dead husband. Yet for this stolen moment, Ryan's to cherish.

He needed to imprint this memory of Anna forever on his brain. It wasn't nearly enough. Not even close to what he longed for. All he'd ever have of Anna, it would need to last him a lifetime.

She gave her child over to him. Gazing at the beautiful baby in his arms, for the second time in his life, Ryan fell in love. Hopelessly, helplessly, irretrievably in love with the bawling creature with the fathomless black eyes.

Although not his child, he felt a love so pure, it took his breath. His vision blurred. *How can this be, God?* But it was so. His heart was hers.

"Welcome to our world, sweet Ruby." He pressed his cheek against the softness of her black curls. "Welcome to our world."

Holding the precious child in his arms, at last he understood the math Canyon Collier had spoken of. The divine equation of love multiplied.

Shifting his weight from side to side, he crooned a lullaby and rocked her gently. "… Angels watching, e'er around thee, All through the night."

Ruby stopped crying as if somehow she recognized his voice. Everything and everyone in the room faded. Her baby fist flailed from beneath the cover and grazed his lips.

"… Soft the drowsy hours are creeping, hill and vale in slumber sleeping." His arms tightened around the drowsy infant.

The child he'd come to love. An unexpected love for a baby who wasn't his. An unexplainable love. A love to which he was ready to devote his life. But Anna had been crystal clear. There was no place for him in her life or Ruby's.

"I my loved ones' watch am keeping…" His voice hitched. "All through the night…" he whispered.

How far was Ryan's love willing to go for Anna and this baby? For him, God's love had been willing to go all the way from heaven to the manger to the cross. Now Ryan had arrived at his own cross. And because of God's love, Ryan's love for Anna and this baby could do no less.

He must love them enough to let them go.

Anna's brown eyes gleamed with bittersweet tears. "Ryan…"

His gaze fell to the sleeping child. "Someone else should have a turn. Goodbye, Anna."

Ryan brushed his lips against the smooth perfection of Ruby's forehead. Inhaling her sweet baby scent, he whispered goodbye as he lowered Ruby into her mother's arms.

Loving her, he let Ruby go. He let them both go. And walked away. Alone into the night.

Chapter Twenty

Ryan was gone before Anna could stop him. One minute he was there loving her child and the next? He slipped away as Ruby went into the loving embrace of her grandparents.

Anna was exhausted by the time her mother and Evy shooed the menfolk out of the bedroom. No one but Ruby wanted to sleep that night. A night no one would ever forget. A Christmas Eve when love had been born in their hearts and in their home again.

Finally her mother last each family member crept quietly to their own beds. To capture a few hours of sleep before dawn bathed the world in the light of Christmas morning. A Christmas like no other.

And though beyond weary, Anna found herself unable to fall asleep. Filled with wonder and gratitude for the intricately woven child lying beside her on the bed. A blessing. God's reminder of His never-failing love for Anna and for those who would always love her. Ryan, most of all.

Last night when he held Ruby, she'd glimpsed in his eyes the kind of love that never let go. A divine love reflected through the grace note of Ryan's love for her. And for a child who wasn't his.

Until the day she died, a part of her would love Ruby's father. But in Ryan's love, she saw herself, Ruby and a future of which she'd not dared to allow herself to dream.

God's precious gifts to her—Mateo, Ruby. And Ryan.

She gazed at the sleeping child in her arms and wept. Why had she not seen it before? Only through much pain had God brought them to each other.

Ruby's upper lip curved sweetly. Something fierce and strong fluttered in Anna's heart. Ruby had been worth any price. The pain. The grief. The loss.

Through the window, she watched as light flooded the eastern sky. And with poignant insight, she realized she'd been so stubborn. So blind to the incredible beauty of the gifts God had placed within her reach. The supreme gift of Himself.

Joy and hope. The pain of yesterday forgotten as if it had never been. As for Ryan? Her heart swelled. Was it too late? Why had he left?

She couldn't shake that one moment last night when Ruby no longer lay between them, but united them. In faith. In love. In purpose.

In the winter-bare branches of the maples outside the window, birds sang a melody of glorious praise. "Please don't let it be too late, God," she whispered.

She swiped her eyes with her hand. She could no longer deny the truth. From the beginning, Ryan believed in her. Without hope of her ever loving him back.

Ryan could be trusted to love her. Ryan could be trusted to love another man's biological child. Because first and foremost, Ryan had proven how much he loved his God.

Last night in Ryan's eyes, she beheld his heart. And in his heroic, sacrificial love, she'd found an unwavering tower of earthly strength. Safety. A place of rest.

Her Bethlehem.

* * *

When Ryan walked out, he found himself adrift. Nowhere to go. The village remained dark.

His boots crunched over the snow on the green. The storm had blown itself out to sea. The skies were clear.

Inside the darkened sanctuary of the never-locked church, he slipped into the front pew. Moonlight shone through the stained glass windows, bathing him in pools of purple, blue and red. He perched on the edge of the seat. His elbows on his knees. His hands knotted together.

The waxy scent of candles from the candlelight service permeated the air. Only a few hours ago, he'd sat here, celebrating the coming birth of a Savior with family and friends.

It felt more distant, not only in terms of space and time, but in emotional mileage, too. In what for him had become an endless night.

Joy intertwined with sorrow. A night from which he couldn't seem to awaken.

Footfalls sounded on the carpeted aisle.

"Bro?" A solid form dropped beside him on the pew. "Will came back to the station. Told us about the baby. Nobody knew where you'd gone."

He wouldn't have guessed that, of his brothers, Ethan would be the one to go looking for him.

"I'm so sorry, Ryan." Ethan's voice thickened. "I know how much you loved her. Loved them both."

Loved. Past tense. If only that were true.

"I appreciate you checking on me, Eth, but I want to be alone."

"Here's the thing, I don't think you should be alone. Not tonight." He laid his hand on Ryan's shoulder. "Or at least what's left of it."

What was left for Ryan? Nothing. So much for his emotional barricades. Because as it turned out, his was the real at-risk heart.

Ethan's grip tightened. "You're not alone, man. Never." His too-quiet, emotionally locked-up brother who hadn't been the same since he returned from Afghanistan.

Through the long night, his brother kept vigil beside him. And sometime during the night, Ryan made his decision. No more playing it safe.

Head down, he clenched his eyes shut. Shoulders hunched. His heart no longer lay in a research lab. His heart and his future lay with kids like Oscar, Maria and Zander. Even if that future didn't include Anna.

When morning broke, he hauled himself to his feet. "Thanks, man." His voice gruff. "For being here, Eth."

"No problem." Ethan shoulder-butted him. "But just so you know, I'm not cleaning up the horse poop Franklin left in the firehouse. That's on you."

Ryan pushed his glasses along the bridge of his nose and smiled. "Got it."

Ethan lumbered to his feet. "There's a gas-powered range at the station. Luke promised a batch of pancakes." He ran his hand over the blond stubble covering his jaw. "It ain't much. Definitely not the Christmas breakfast we hoped for—"

"But while it's Christmas and we're here," Ryan finished for him, "we might as well eat."

Ethan's mouth curved. "Something like that."

Outside, Kiptohanock lay in a pristine, snow-covered mantle of purity. Undisturbed. Tranquil.

The idea of warm pancakes caused his stomach to growl. But first, he had to make sure one last time that all was well with those he loved most in the world.

"I'll be there soon," he promised as they parted on the steps.

Ethan's brow creased.

"It's okay. Save me a place at the table."

His brother turned toward the station. And Ryan headed in the opposite direction. Slogging his way through the deserted streets.

The village was beginning to stir. There were signs of life as homeowners surveyed the damage from the ice storm. Outside the Coast Guard station, the metal rods of the two flags—American and Coastie—clanged against the flagpole. The flags stretched taut in the stiff sea breeze coming off the harbor.

From a habit nurtured within every 'born here, his gaze flitted toward the barrier islands. Like a string of translucent pearls beneath the bluing of the sky. He gauged the sky and the wind. A calm sea. A good day.

The electric lines hummed. The star on top of the gazebo surged to life. With power restored, faint cheers echoed from the open bay of the firehouse. He rounded the square to Anna's family home.

It might take a while to connect Kiptohanock with the rest of the world again. But life would go on. As it must. As it was always meant to.

He paused in front of the Pruitt house. He meant only to go as far as the porch. Take a quick look and be on his way. He didn't want to intrude. It wasn't his way to force himself where he wasn't wanted. Or needed.

But the steps squeaked as he crept toward the bay window. Inside, the multicolored lights of the Christmas tree glowed. Glittering foil-wrapped presents lay underneath the tree. And on the sofa, Anna held the sleeping child in her arms.

His Adam's apple bobbed. She swaddled her daughter in the soft blanket old Mrs. Evans had made for Kiptohanock's Christmas baby.

Ryan must've made an inadvertent movement. Anna's head snapped up, her eyes meeting his outside the window. Her lips parted. He froze, locked in place. Lost in her brown eyes.

She mouthed something to him. The baby stirred. Anna motioned him toward the door.

Freed from his paralysis, he entered the foyer and toed out of his boots. He padded into the living room.

"I'd kiss you right now—" her lips quivered "—except I can't reach you."

He glanced up, finding himself standing underneath the sprig of glossy green mistletoe.

Anna rose from the couch and winced.

He rushed forward. "You shouldn't be on your feet."

"Please don't leave." Easing onto the sofa, she patted the cushion beside her. "Sit with me, Ryan."

Sounds filtered from upstairs.

"Charlie got home a few hours ago. He carried the baby and me downstairs." She chewed her lip. "When are you leaving for North Carolina?"

He lifted his chin. "I decided not to take the job in North Carolina. I'm going to accept the job with the intervention program and stay in Kiptohanock."

"Ryan..." She held out her hand. "Please come and talk to me."

Never able to refuse Anna anything, he took a slow step toward her.

"I discovered something last night after you left, Ryan."

He took another step closer. "What's that, Anna?"

"It *is* darkest before the dawn."

His heart had to be pounding out of his chest. Surely Ruby would hear it and awaken. "What do you mean?"

"I was terrified I'd never see you again. That I'd lost you for good."

He sat down. "I will always be your friend."

"My first and best friend." She leaned closer. "But my heart yearns for more." She dropped her eyes. "I didn't mean those things I said to you yesterday before the storm."

What was she saying? Could she possibly mean what he hoped? But if any possibility existed that one day she would return his love, he'd wait for Anna forever.

"I'll be here for you." His voice sounded as ragged as his heart felt. "As long as you need me."

She blinked, her eyelashes spiky with tears. "That's just it, Ryan. I don't need you." Her gaze cut to the lights on the tree.

Pain knifed through Ryan. He drew back, but she captured his hand.

"I don't need you, but I desperately want you in my life and Ruby's."

He couldn't tear his eyes from her face.

"I love you, Ryan." She made a sound, a half sob. "Totally. Completely. Helplessly."

"But you said…" Insecurity gnawed at Ryan. "What about your husband?"

"I wasn't being truthful to you or myself. I didn't want you to give up your dream because of me. The past was just an excuse because I was afraid if I admitted I loved you, I'd get hurt again."

Like a dormant seed buried deep in the cold earth of winter, hope surged to the surface of his heart. "You love me?"

"Could you find it in your heart to give me another chance to show you how much…?" Tears ran down her cheeks. "How very much I love you."

He caught one tear on the tip of his finger, where it glistened like morning dew.

"I want to spend the rest of my life with you," she said.

"Wherever your dreams take you. I know how much you want to return to your research."

He swallowed. "Dreams have a way of changing when there's something you want more. My dream has become working with the at-risk children. Being part of your baby's life."

"Ruby's not just mine." Anna handed the sleeping child into his open arms. "You are her father in the truest sense of the word."

Nestling Ruby in the crook of his arm, he lifted a strand of hair off Anna's cheek. Fingering its silky texture.

"Ryan..." she breathed. "Say something. Tell me I haven't ruined this precious, beautiful thing God has done for us."

His palm cupped her cheek. Her skin warmed his hand. Sending electrical sparks straight to his heart.

The love he hardly dared to believe shone from her deep brown eyes. Love for him. A love he scarcely could believe she offered him.

"I love you so much, Anna."

Was this where I fit into Your plan all along, God?

He moved his hand behind the nape of her neck. Tenderly, softly, his lips met Anna's. The baby stirred but settled with a contented sigh. His baby. His Anna. His most precious love.

God was good. A happily-ever-after more wonderful than he could've dared dream. Anna loving him. This baby in his arms wrapped in a Christmas joy that he'd forever hold in his heart.

"Will you promise to grow old with me, Anna?" he whispered.

"As long as the Lord allows." Her eyes were dewy. "The best is still yet to be, my darling." She clung to him. Holding him close. Holding their love close.

Ryan would get to be a fundamental part of who Ruby Reyes would become. Her first words. First steps. Birthdays. Other Christmases.

He rested his forehead against Anna. "Of course, this means certain prerequisites must be taken care of."

A smile teased the corners of her mouth. "Would this involve Reverend Parks?"

"Your brothers, too. The whole town of Kiptohanock. Whatever you want."

A wistful look crossed her face. "My dad would love to give me away this time."

Ryan held his two great loves close to his heart. "Whenever you're ready. A church wedding."

She tilted her head. "How would you feel about a romantic wedding in the gazebo?"

Ryan nodded. "We can wait for the weather to warm come spring."

Her eyes flickered. "On second thought, I don't think I want to wait that long."

"Can't be soon enough for me." His voice went husky. "How about we pray for a balmy Valentine's Day?"

A smile flitted across her lips. "I like how you think, Mr. Savage." She cocked her head toward the window. "Did you hear that?"

He caught the melodious strain ringing from the steeple on this crisp December morning. "Bells."

Ruby lay across both their laps.

Anna gave him a tremulous smile. "Christmas bells."

It seemed fitting to Ryan that their love story should unfold on the day of their Savior's birth. God's love story for all mankind.

She stroked the dark hair on her daughter's head. "Ruby and I are home in Kiptohanock with our family. But most of all, my dearest love, we're home with you."

Chimes rang out across the village. A herald resounding through the ages. A never-ending proclamation of peace on earth.

His beloved Christmas baby stretched, her little heel coming out from the blanket. Her big, brown eyes opened and fastened onto his face. Cradling his child, he dreamed of glorious days to come.

And gave thanks for the day Love made Ryan's heart His home.

* * * * *

If you loved this tale of sweet romance,
pick up these other stories
from author Lisa Carter

COAST GUARD COURTSHIP
COAST GUARD SWEETHEART
FALLING FOR THE SINGLE DAD
THE DEPUTY'S PERFECT MATCH
THE BACHELOR'S UNEXPECTED FAMILY

Available now from Love Inspired!

Find more great reads at www.LoveInspired.com

Dear Reader,

Sometimes we find love. And sometimes, like an unexpected gift, love finds us.

In writing this story, I was forced to ask myself, how far was I willing to go for love? What would I sacrifice? What would I risk?

To risk much for love, like Anna, I have to be willing to come to the end of my pride and self-sufficiency if I am to discover God's best, often unexpected, gift for me. Like Ryan, I, too, have grappled with what this kind of love will cost me. Sometimes I lacked the courage to love this way—feeling the cost too high. The price of obedience. The cost of laying down my plans. The death of self.

But love is a choice. An unconditional love with no expectation of return demands courage. My prayer—like Ryan's—is for God's love to be born in me so that I might love the way God loves us. And to persevere in loving, despite knowing the outcome may never be what I long for most—but trusting God anyway.

Bethlehem and Calvary are *the* greatest love story. God's love story for all mankind when He chose to make our heart His home. Love is calling, and I pray you will answer love's call.

I hope you have enjoyed taking this Christmas journey with me, Anna and Ryan. I would love to hear from you. You may email me at lisa@lisacarterauthor.com or visit www.lisacarterauthor.com.

Wishing you fair winds and following seas,
Lisa Carter

COMING NEXT MONTH FROM
Love Inspired®

Available December 19, 2017

AN AMISH ARRANGEMENT
Amish Hearts • by Jo Ann Brown
Hoping to make his dream of owning a farm come true, Jeremiah Stoltzfus clashes with Mercy Bamberger, who believes the land belongs to her. When Mercy becomes foster mom to a young boy who only Jeremiah seems to reach, suddenly their mission becomes clear. But will their hearts open for each other?

THE TEXAN'S TWINS
Lone Star Legacy • by Jolene Navarro
Reid McAllister is surprised to find the wildlife sanctuary where he's doing community service is run by Danica Bergmann, the wife he left behind—and that he's the father of twin daughters he didn't know he had! Now he's determined to help Danica keep her dream alive—and earn her trust in their family's happiness.

CLAIMING HER COWBOY
Big Heart Ranch • by Tina Radcliffe
Jackson Harris never thought investigating Big Heart Ranch's claim to be a haven for orphaned children would turn him into a temporary cowboy—or that he'd be falling for adorable triplets and the ranch director! Lucy Maxwell's plan to put the city lawyer through the wringer also goes awry as she's roped in by his charm and caring ways.

A MOM FOR HIS DAUGHTER
by Jean C. Gordon
Discovering she has a niece who's been adopted, Fiona Bryce seeks to get to know the little girl. Widowed single dad Marc Delacroix isn't sure he can trust that Fiona won't seek custody. Neither imagined that caring for three-year-old Stella would lead to a chance at a forever family.

HER HANDYMAN HERO
Home to Dover • by Lorraine Beatty
Reid Blackthorn promised his brother he'd keep an eye on his niece—so he takes a job as handyman with Lily's guardian. Tori Montgomery hired Reid to help with repairs to her B and B, never expecting she'd develop feelings for him. But can their relationship survive when she discovers his secret?

INSTANT FAMILY
by Donna Gartshore
Single mom Frankie Munro is looking for a fresh start—she has no time for romance. But when she and her daughter rent a lakeside cottage, next-door neighbor Ben Cedar makes it difficult to stick to those plans. As neighbors turn to friends, will camaraderie turn to love?

LICNM1217

Get 2 Free Books,
Plus 2 Free Gifts—
just for trying the Reader Service!

LI17R2

1 M

Inspirational Romance to Warm Your Heart and Soul

Join our social communities to connect with other readers who share your love!

Sign up for the Love Inspired newsletter at **www.LoveInspired.com** to be the first to find out about upcoming titles, special promotions and exclusive content.

CONNECT WITH US AT:

Harlequin.com/Community

 Facebook.com/LoveInspiredBooks

 Twitter.com/LoveInspiredBks

LISOCIAL2017